‘

Fancy ⊔⊔⊔⊔⊔ ⊔⊔⊔ ⊔⊔⊔⊔⊔.

A Christian mystery

By Maxine Holmgren

Copyright

Cover, internal design and preparation for publication by Mark S. Fletcher www.JABOP.com.

For assistance in preparing your next book for publication contact: **PrepMyBook@jabop.com**

Acknowledgment

Thanks to my wonderful husband who gave me the time, space and encouragement to write.

Thanks to family and friends who also encouraged me.

Thanks to all the Mystery Tea Party fans who sent me emails and pictures of their mystery tea parties, and said "Keep Writing."

Special thanks to Mark Fletcher, who had the knowledge, expertise and patience to turn my pages into an actual book, and design the front cover.

Chapter 1

I knew I shouldn't have gone with my sister, Liz, to the old, deserted Harwood mansion. Even the long, secluded driveway was creepy. Overgrown bushes seemed to reach out and claw at her red Ferrari, as we inched along the bumpy, gravel lane.

"The bank knows darn well if they want to get rid of this Harwood monstrosity quickly, I'm the best realtor to do it," Liz bragged as she maneuvered over a rut the size of a canyon.

And she was right. She knew the real estate business inside out. She and her third husband, Roger, owned River Home Realty. She was the top award winning agent in the whole county.

She was the aggressive, outgoing sister. I was the quiet, reserved one. Our opposite personalities made the perfect sister team, as we balanced each other. We were opposite in looks, too. I was slim and athletic; Liz was almost twice my size, without an athletic bone in her large frame. We both visited Miss Clairol regularly. I favored the blonde shades to bring life to my mousy brown hair, while Liz purchased red colors.

"I told the bank president I'd have a buyer for this white elephant before the ink is dry on the foreclosure papers," she said, as the fabled mansion loomed into sight.

Murder at the Fancy Frills Tea Room

It had been a magnificent showplace in its heyday. Now it stood neglected, unwanted, and foreboding. Broken glass and debris from recent storms covered the sagging wrap around porch. Boarded up windows, shutters that were about to fall off and gaping holes in the porch were all that was left of the renowned mansion.

"Come on, let's see if we can get in," she said as she parked the car.

"You said you had a key!" I was beginning to understand that premonition of disaster I'd been feeling. Anxiety had been sitting on my shoulder like a vulture, ever since I'd let Liz talk me into accompanying her to see the inside of the infamous old house.

I admit I'd always wanted see the interior of the place. Rumors were that there were gold faucets in the bathrooms and Italian marble in the foyer. It was said that one room had a home movie screen that covered a whole wall. Silent movie stars had enjoyed seeing their latest releases there, while sipping champagne. That was before the house had been sold to a famous gangster from prohibition days. I'd been told stories about underground tunnels that led to the river. Bootleg liquor was transported by night into the mansion. Legend had it that more than one mobster, that had visited the mansion, never made it out alive. I shivered at the thought of what secrets the old place held.

We made our way around to the back of the house, avoiding broken tree limbs, branches and other debris, trying to peer through gaps in the boarded up windows.

"Liz, you invited me to a tour of the place. Didn't the bank give you a key?"

"Of course they gave me a key," she answered, to my relief. "I've just misplaced it, that's all. But, no problem. Look, I think this board is loose." With that, she began prying it loose, applying all the strength her 5'10, 200 pound figure could muster. The weather beaten boards were no match for her, and immediately gave way, exposing a window.

"Where there's a will, there's a way," she grinned. She stepped back and looked around. "That'll do just fine!" She picked up a huge rock.

"You can't do that!" I protested. "You'll get us arrested. What you have in mind is called breaking and entering."

"In the real estate business, it's called getting ahead of the competition." She dropped the rock inside her Samsonite size purse and swung it at the window. The glass shattered as the old dried wood frame easily broke away, leaving a gaping entry into the house. "Give me a leg up," she directed.

At this point, anyone in their right mind would have run for their lives. But all my life I have done whatever my big sister told me to do, and those "old tapes" kicked in. Once more, I followed her instructions. And once more, she got me into trouble.

I hoisted her ample frame in an upward motion the best I could. After all, she outweighed me by a good 70 pounds! When she seemed to hang momentarily half way in and half way out, I just gave her a good shove. The result was a loud thud and a groan as she landed on the floor, inside the house.

The sight of Liz's ample posterior wiggling through the window, panty-hosed legs flailing in the air for balance, was one that would stick in my memory for a long time. I wonder if sounds stick in the memory as well. Like the sound of the security system screaming in my ears?

The back door flew open, and Liz pulled me inside. Her red realtor blazer was covered with dust but she looked proud of herself.

I was amazed at how fast the Sheriff's Dept. arrived. Liz was still pounding on the alarm box, trying to silence it, when I saw two squad cars barreling down the long driveway. Their screeching sirens added to the deafening noise assaulting my ears. The police cars roared to a stop, and four officers leaped out, with guns drawn.

I was terrified. Not Liz. She opened the door and cheerily waved to the approaching policemen. "It's alright, Sheriff. No cause for alarm. It's just me and Emily, everything's OK."

Sheriff Doyle actually looked disappointed to discover the break-in was only caused by two local females. I'm sure he was hoping to capture some notorious criminals to boost his image in the upcoming election. He gave her a dirty look as he strode past into the house and did something to the security box.

Ah, silence. I breathed a sigh of relief and gave the Sheriff my best smile of innocence.

"Have a look around outside, men. See if any more damage has been done to the property." He eyed the broken glass on the floor.

"Now I know what you're thinking, Sheriff, but it's not the way it looks," I tried to explain. "Liz is actually working with the bank. Right, Liz?" I turned the explanation over to her.

"That's right; I'm going to sell this place for the bank. They gave me a key, but when we got here I discovered I'd left it at the office. I didn't want to run all the way back to town to get it." She looked at me. "It would have made Emily late to open her tea shop. She was so anxious to see the inside of the mansion, I just couldn't disappoint her."

I could see where Sis was going with this. She would make it appear to be all my fault, and she would be the heroine for figuring out a way to please me and still get me back to open up the shop on time. I tried to look demure and smiled at the Sheriff.

"So, I thought if I broke that little old kitchen window, and shimmied through, I could let Emily in, show her around, take her back to town, and have the window replaced before anyone would ever know." She shrugged her shoulders, "And no harm done. Unfortunately, someone forgot to tell me about the security alarm."

That's when I noticed the awkward way she was standing, kind of leaning to one side as she talked. It seemed her skirt was wrapped snuggly around her legs, and she leaned against the old kitchen range to keep it that way. Surely she couldn't be cold; it was a beautiful spring day. I glanced at the Sheriff, and followed his gaze to the broken window. A remnant of Liz's skirt waved like a flagship banner from a piece of jagged glass.

"Well, Liz, that may all be well and true, but I'm gonna have to take you and Emily down to the station while I fill out some reports and check on your story. You ladies come with me and I'll have Bear drive your car back to town." Bear was the nickname people in town had given Sgt. Brown, because of his hulking size.

Murder at the Fancy Frills Tea Room

The Sheriff held the back door open for us. Liz waited for me to move, and then popped right in front of me. I had a hard time not laughing out loud when I realized her predicament, and why she had been standing in such an awkward position. Her skirt had a huge three corner tear that looked a lot like the trap door in long underwear. She was trying to hold it together with one hand in back of her, and hold on to her huge bag and realtor notebooks with the other. The heavy rock, still in her bag, wasn't helping her equilibrium. One of the heels of her Gucci shoes had broken off, and she hobbled ungracefully toward the squad car.

I did my best not to giggle and followed closely behind her, trying to provide cover for her exposed derriere. Once more, I felt like I was playing Ethel to her Lucy.

✱✱✱✱✱

I'd never been in a squad car before. It smelled of coffee, leather, and some other strong scent I couldn't place. Probably best not to know!

Liz climbed in, and as soon as she sat down began rummaging in her bag. Seconds later, she dug out her cell phone and began texting.

"You and your "I forgot the key", I mimicked. "I bet you lost it, didn't you? You're always losing things," I complained. "What if we get arrested? I'll never live it down. I can see the headlines now, "Owner of Fancy Frills Tea Room Arrested for Breaking and Entering."

"Oh, don't worry. You won't be arrested. Everything is under control. Besides, think of the free publicity you could get if you made the headlines. Customers would flock to the shop to see if it were true." She dropped the cell phone back in her bag, a look of satisfaction on her face.

Leave it to Liz to make lemonade out of lemons. Then I remembered something my Pastor had once said. 'Try to find at least four good things about any troubling situation you find yourself in, and be thankful for them.' I began counting. 1. We hadn't been hand-cuffed. 2. We were in a nice, safe police car. 3. We knew Sheriff Doyle and Bear personally. Number 4 took some thought but I finally came up with the fact that Liz hadn't been hurt climbing through the window.

I felt better once I became thankful for my blessings.

When we got to the police station, none other than the bank President, Phillip Barker, was waiting for us. He was one of those men who got more distinguished looking as he got older. His full head of hair was just beginning to gray at the temples. His mustache was neatly trimmed, and there wasn't a wrinkle in his dark blue business suit.

He looked every inch the professional banker, so why was he acting more upset than we?

"Are you alright? What a terrible experience for you!" he exclaimed as he helped Liz to a chair in the Sheriff's office. He ignored me completely, focusing entirely on Liz. "Have you hurt your ankle?" He was actually wringing his hands!

I sat down in a metal chair against the wall. No one seemed to notice me anyway.

"Sheriff, how could you treat one of the town's most respected citizens like this?" Philip demanded.

The Sheriff took his seat of authority behind his big wooden desk, covered with file folders, papers and an assortment of empty fast food cartons and Styrofoam cups. He glared at the bank president. "She says you gave her a key and that she had the banks OK to be out there."

"Well, yes, of course, that's exactly right." Phillip glanced at Liz approvingly. "She's going to find a buyer for the old Harwood place."

There was something phony about his smile and his voice. He was nodding in agreement with everything Liz told the Sheriff about our misadventure. I think he would have agreed if she had said the bank was going to turn the old mansion into a hotel for aliens from outer space. I couldn't wait to get Liz alone and find out what bit of information she was holding over his head to turn this pompous snob into an agreeable ally.

"Can I get you water, coffee – anything, my dear?" He hovered over Liz. I was still invisible.

Finally, after Phillip made it clear he would not press charges, the Sheriff told us we could go. Rather, he told Liz she could go, and then nodded in my direction.

Phillip held her arm as she marched triumphantly out of the station. But she forgot to hold her skirt closed, and her mini slip, now hiked up around her hips, revealed torn panty hose and pink lace panties. A brisk spring breeze left little to the imagination.

Chapter 2

I woke early the next morning and had a wonderful time of prayer and bible reading. I read a chapter of Proverbs every morning; 31 days in a month, 31 proverbs. No matter how many times I read Proverbs, there's always something new for me. This morning, I even took time to sit quietly and listen. Prayer is supposed to be a time of communion with God, a conversation. But I seem to do all the talking, so I've been trying to get in the habit of sitting and listening, too. Sometimes I hear God's voice, not audibly, of course, but in my heart. This morning I heard him say "Trust me in all that lies ahead." Sounds good to me, Lord, I thought. I went glibly on my way.

When I got to the tea shop, I found my partner, Pat, busy doing two things at once. She had fancy scones baking in the big commercial oven and was mixing dough for her delightful Angel Wing cookies. She almost looked like an angel herself, wearing her white smock and white baker's hat.

When she spoke, that image vanished. "You'll have to get the flowers yourself, that kid they got doin' deliveries didn't show up this morning."

"Good Morning to you, too," I greeted her. "Hope Jimmy's not sick."

Murder at the Fancy Frills Tea Room

Pat had served in the military as a cook, and then as a chef at a high-class resort. That was a good thing for the business, but not so good for me. She pulled rank on me and issued orders like a top sergeant.

"Nah, Probably a case of spring fever." She looked up from her work. "Can you run to the store and get frozen orange juice concentrate? I want to make chocolate chip/orange scones today."

"Sure," I replied. I put my purse under the counter, and began to collect the teapots that served as vases from the tables in the tea room. It had been my idea to use cracked teapots or those that had lost their lids as flower filled centerpieces. I loved the feminine ambience of the tea room, all the fancy frills, though Pat thought it completely unnecessary.

I unlocked the back door and took the dead flowers out to the trash bin. Arthur, from the antique shop next door, was already there, breaking down cardboard boxes.

"How's the pretty tea lady today?" he greeted me.

"Good Morning, Arthur. I'm fine." I decided to have a little fun with him. "You'll never guess where I've been this morning."

"Let me think." He stroked his neatly trimmed beard for a second, thoughtfully. "A respectable, church going lady like you, wouldn't have been out at the old Harwood mansion...and arrested for trespassing, would you?"

My mouth dropped. "How in the world did you hear about that?"

"Oh, I have my ways of keeping track of you, dear." He leaned toward me. "You know how I feel about you."

I stepped back, embarrassed. I was never sure if Arthur's flirting was meaningful or not. He seemed to be happily married to Sue, so I was fairly certain he was just trying to boost my morale.

"So, what trouble did Liz get you into this time?" He stuffed more cardboard into the big, green dumpster.

I plucked out a few mums and daisies that still looked perky and dropped the rest of the wilted flowers into the trash.

"Well, I've always wanted to see the inside of the Harwood mansion. I've heard so much about it. You know all the stories of movie stars and gangsters from long ago, the glitz and glamour of the place. So, when Liz told me she was going out there to look around, so she could sell the place for the bank, I wanted to go too. I couldn't refuse her invitation! But when we got out there, she'd forgotten the key. She's always forgetting things."

Arthur laughed. "I can see where this is going."

"Next thing I know, she's broken a window and has me help her climb in. That set off the security alarm, and in minutes the Sheriff was there with two police cars!"

"I heard the two of you were brought back to town in the squad car. And that Phillip Barker was waiting at the station to press charges against you. What happened?" Arthur asked.

"When I saw Phillip at the Police Station my heart sank. I thought for sure we were really in trouble," I recalled.

"You mean he didn't press charges? I can't believe that. He's such a pompous jerk." Arthur let the cover to the dumpster drop with a bang.

"I know, I was surprised, too." I agreed. "Actually, he was very nice about it all. He couldn't do enough to clear us and get us out of there quickly. I'm just so thankful he was so understanding."

At that moment, Sue called from their back door. "Telephone, Arthur. It's about the music boxes you ordered."

I watched him as he sprinted over to his shop. I couldn't help but envy Sue for having a husband like Arthur. He was tall, nice looking and fun to be with. I wondered if she appreciated her blessings. It's a good thing Pat's loud voice interrupted my thoughts, before I started feeling lonely and sorry for myself again.

"I need that o.j. today," she said gruffly.

"On my way," I answered. How I wished I could buy Pat out and be the sole owner of my precious tea room. Pretty sad when the love of your life is a tea room instead of a man!

"Hi, Emily, Top Sarge giving you orders again?" Betty popped open the back door to her boutique and waved a dust cloth at me.

This alley was getting more business than the shops! I waved back and ducked into the kitchen, before Betty could ask me any questions about whatever she might have heard about my morning adventure. The flowers would have to wait. The scripture "This is the day the Lord has made; Let us rejoice and be glad in it," came to my mind. (Ps.118:24 NIV). I hoped the rest of the day would be fairly quiet. Little did I know.

I slipped through the back door and checked the refrigerator to see what else I might need, and began making a list. "How are you doing today?" I asked my busy partner.

"I'll let you know later," she said, "Trina's coming by today. I know what she wants. More money."

I didn't know what to say. Sometimes there doesn't seem to be a proper response.

Pat continued talking while adding things to a mixing bowl. "I don't mind helping my daughter out. I've always done that. Kinda makes up for all the time I was gone, in the service, you know. But something's wrong." She stopped what she was doing, and shook her head. "Something's fishy. I'm worried about Trina. Have you seen her lately? She looks terrible. She's let herself go, and lost a lot of weight. And she's started running around with a bad bunch. That boyfriend of hers is nothing but trouble. Every time she sees me, she wants more money."

I suddenly understood why Pat had seemed so distraught and moody lately. She must be worried sick about her daughter. Pat might be a tough old ex-army sergeant, but she still had a Mother's heart.

"I'm sorry to hear this, Pat," I said. "Is there anything I can do?"

She picked up her spatula and began scraping the bowl. "Well, maybe you can say a few prayers for me and Trina. You know God a lot better than I do."

"He wants you to know him, too," I replied. "He loves you very much, and Trina, too."

A loud banging on the door announced the arrival of UPS. I hurried to open the door and sign for the delivery. Pat turned the radio down and gruffly called out that she really needed the grocery items right away.

Another lost chance to tell her about Jesus, I thought, as I headed out the door, list in hand. As I hurried down the street, a white Cadillac convertible pulled up alongside me.

"Hey, watch it, lady. There's a speed limit on that sidewalk. We have to maintain the image of a quaint, sleepy village with a low stress level," Liz's husband, Roger called out.

I stepped to the side of the car. "On your way to the golf course?"

"What was your first clue? The clubs in the back seat?" He glanced in the rear view mirror.

"I have God's gift of discernment," I laughed. "Where's Liz?"

"I thought maybe you'd know," he said, "Hard to keep up with her. If she's not listing a property, she's closing a deal, or holding an open house. I left her a message on her cell phone that'd I'd be at the Lakes Country Club. Might even find someone that wants to buy or sell a house while I'm playing golf." He waved good-bye and was off.

Roger was retired, and only dabbled in the real estate business. He'd gotten his realtors license to please Liz, but his passion and pleasure in life was golf. He was one of those rare people who were actually good at it. He liked to joke that he was a scratch golfer, and that Liz kept him scratching.

✳✳✳✳✳

I completed my errands and headed back to the shop. Fresh flowers in one hand, and balancing a paper bag of groceries in the other, I wiggled my way through the back door. I stopped by the old refrigerator in the back hall that we use to store things, and placed the flowers inside. I wanted them to stay fresh until I had time to arrange them. I stopped in my tracks when I heard angry voices.

"You've got to help me, Mom!" I recognized Trina's voice at once.

"Enough is enough! What'd you do with the last thousand I loaned you? Loan! Ha! Fat chance I'll ever see that money again!"

"Mom, you don't understand. I gotta have this. "

"Look at you, skinny as a rail. Come home for a while," Pat pleaded. "Stay with me and get some good home cookin 'in ya, and get your life straightened out."

"No, I can't do that. Please. I'm desperate. I gotta have the money." Trina was crying now, begging. It sounded like she was begging for her life. "Please, please. I'll pay you back, I promise I will."

"I've heard enough of your promises. I won't give you another penny."

"You better come through, if you know what's good for you, and for Trina." A man's voice spoke harshly.

"You keep out of this," Pat yelled.

Should I step in? I didn't mean to be eavesdropping, but I couldn't help overhearing their argument.

Murder at the Fancy Frills Tea Room

"If you know what's good for you, you'll give her the $10,000," the man's voice said.

Ten thousand! If my mouth had dropped any further open it would have crashed on the floor, giving away my presence.

"Are you threatening me?" Pat demanded.

"She's gonna get your money when you die anyway," the man's voice had a deadly ring to it. "Why not save yourself the trouble, and give it to her now?"

I never noticed that the wet celery had leaked through the grocery bag, weakening the brown paper fibers. The bottom of the bag gave way, and the celery slipped right through onto the floor. Cans of frozen concentrate followed, rolling every which way.

"Oh, clumsy me." I stooped down to retrieve celery and orange juice cans. When I looked up, I saw Pat and a woman I hardly recognized as Pat's daughter, Trina. A big man with dark hair and scruffy beard scowled at me.

"Sorry to interrupt," I tried to act innocent. "What's going on?" I looked from one angry face to another.

"Nothing. They were just leaving," Pat said.

"How long were you out there?" the mouth in the beard demanded.

"I, uh, I just came in." I tried to smile. "Darn grocery bags aren't like they used to be. I should have asked for plastic."

"Remember what I said," the man glared at Pat. "We'll be in touch." He half led, half shoved Trina through the door. "We'll be in touch," he repeated emphatically.

I watched Trina wipe her eyes as they got into the old truck parked at the curb.

"I hardly recognized Trina," I told Pat. "You were right. She doesn't look well. She's lost a lot of weight."

"Just how long were you out there?" Pat asked.

"Long enough," I put my arm around her shoulder. "Are you alright? You look pretty shook up."

"I don't want to talk about it," she shrugged my arm off her shoulder. "I've got scones to make."

Chapter 3

It all started with the UPS man. I had barely finished signing for the packages when Pat came into the tea room from the kitchen. She had a large metal spoon with a heavy black handle in her hand, and she pointed at the packages with it as she talked.

"What's all this?" she demanded. "I told you not to go crazy buying stuff. We don't need any more of that junk! I'm not made of money."

I took a deep breath and made a conscious effort to keep my voice calm, as I once more explained, "If we're going to make any money, we have to have things to sell, besides food. Customers expect to see tea things; china tea cups and saucers, silver compotes, sugar tongs, and tea cozies." I held up some cheerful Mary Englebreit cards for her to see, hoping the bright colors would brighten her mood.

"Send 'em back," she growled. "Tell them we don't want them."

"You mean you don't want them. Don't you see, Pat, we have to have things in our display cases. It adds to the ambiance."

Why do I always want to cry when I get angry or frustrated? Then I get angry at myself for crying. I could feel the tears welling up. I willed myself to get a hold on my emotions.

I silently prayed, *"Lord, give me your love for Pat, and wisdom."* I knew she was upset over the incident I'd just witnessed, but she was always difficult to work with. I'd been trying to understand and love Pat ever since we had become partners. She had seemed like an answer to my prayers at the time, providing the money and cooking expertise for the tea room. I had the business head and the dream for a tea room. Now my dream was to buy Pat out. If only I had the money.

I continued opening the packages, unwrapping delicate flowered china teacups and saucers. They would be irresistible on the little corner table among the tussie-mussies and lavender scented sachets.

"The ladies that come in here look for more than a cup of tea or a sandwich," I explained to Pat. "They long to be surrounded by pretty things. There's something in our soul that longs for beauty and tranquility. All these little lovelies add to the setting, and makes their time here more enjoyable. When they leave, they want to take a piece of it with them so they buy a box of note cards or a pretty dish for themselves or for a gift. We can add a good forty to sixty percent to our sales with these add-ons."

I was saved from further argument from Pat by the bell on the door as Pastor Steve rushed through the front door.

Pat mumbled something under her breath and returned to her domain, the kitchen.

"Emily, I just heard the news. I couldn't believe it! They told me you had been arrested!" His eyes were filled with concern.

News traveled faster in Riverbend than a penguin on ice.

"It was nothing, Pastor, really." I could feel my face turning red. How embarrassing for me; a lady deacon at the church, to have my Pastor think I was some sort of a criminal! Wait till I get my hands on Liz! I just might commit a criminal offense!

"I heard you were captured at the Harwood Place and that it took the man power from two squad cars to get you out. They said you were seen being taken into custody in hand cuffs, and that your sister was so drunk she couldn't walk straight." He placed his hands on his hips, waiting for an explanation.

I couldn't help it, I burst out laughing. "Oh, my goodness, is that what you thought? It wasn't like that at all."

He looked relieved, and I pointed to a chair.

"Sit down and let me get you a cup of chamomile tea, and I'll tell you all about it; the truth, the whole truth, and nothing but the truth." I hoped the calming effects of this particular tea would reduce the Pastor's stress over the rumors he'd heard about me.

After I explained everything to him, and he'd finished the tea and cranberry scone I'd served him, he looked peaceful again, and patted his pocket.

"I brought my check book. I knew there'd be a reasonable explanation, and I was prepared to post bond for you, if necessary." He smiled. "I'm glad the only check I'll have to write will be for a gift for my wife. Help me find a birthday present for Nancy, will you? Has she been eyeing anything special in your store lately?"

Murder at the Fancy Frills Tea Room

"Oh, you want to buy a gift for your wife?" I repeated in a voice loud enough for Pat to hear. "She was admiring this tea set the other day."

Pastor Steve wrote the check and I gift wrapped the present for him. As he headed out the door, he said "I want to stop at the hospital and see Fred. Martha says he's not doing too well."

"Sorry to hear that. I'll send some of his favorite scones and some flowers over," I promised. "See you at the church council meeting this evening."

Ladies began arriving for the noon lunch a bit earlier than usual. I bustled about, putting the UPS parcels in the back room, some opened, and some still unopened. I loved getting deliveries. Sometimes I forget what I've ordered, and opening the packages was almost as much fun as Christmas.

Liz picked the busiest minute of the lunch hour to burst through the door like a whirlwind.

"Emily!" She grabbed my arm and I almost dropped the teapot I had just filled. She dragged me back to the side alcove, near the back of the room, close to the kitchen.

"Liz, I have to serve this cinnamon plum tea to table number three. The ladies are waiting," I complained, trying to break free from her grasp. Then I noticed her face was an ashen shade of grey. And it wasn't just a new shade of foundation that she was trying out. Her hand trembled as she clutched my arm.

"You'll never guess what I just found out." She didn't wait for me to answer. "They found a body out there."

"What? Out where? Whose body?" The questions tumbled out, without thinking, as fast as they formed in my mind. Then I realized Liz was in no condition to answer questions until she calmed down.

"Here, sit down and drink this." I poured a cup of the cinnamon plum tea for her. "I'll be right back." As much as I wanted to hear the news, business was business, and the ladies at table three were still waiting.

I poured tea for the ladies and made cheerful small talk, about the many benefits of herbal tea, with Liz's news churning in the background of my mind. I hurried back to Liz. The color was returning to her face, and she was talking to Pat. Now Pat was the one with the ashen face as she watched Liz make stabbing motions with her upraised arm.

"Do they know who he was?" Pat asked.

"Not a clue," Liz answered. She turned to me. "Wait till you hear what happened." I could tell she was feeling better, and warming up to being the bearer of exciting news. I motioned to Marcie, our part time helper, to take care of the last of the luncheon crowd and sat down at the chintz covered table. Liz took a sip of her tea and began.

"Remember this morning, when we were out at the Harwood place?"

"As if I could forget! What's that got to do with anything?"

Liz leaned forward as she explained. "Well, when we left in the Sheriff's car, the rest of the cops stayed there, remember? They said they had to secure the building – whatever that means. I think they just wanted to take a gander at those gold bathroom fixtures."

Murder at the Fancy Frills Tea Room

She drained her tea cup. "I heard they spent quite a bit of time looking the place over, the cook's tour, you know, and they were just ready to leave when somebody thought of the basement. They hadn't checked it out. So, Bear sent Harley. "

"At first Harley, you know Harley, he's been on the force so long he's gotten slow. He has arthritis, you know. So he didn't want to go down there, on account of the steps. But Bear pulled rank on him and made him go. So, Harley worked his way down, and when Bear heard him yell, he went flying down to see what was the matter. He was probably feeling guilty for making that poor old man go down those steep steps all alone, into that dark, scary basement."

"You digress!" I said impatiently. "Just give me the Readers Digest condensed version. What did they find down there?" I kept one eye on the lunch room, making sure Marcie could handle the customers that still dwindled in, as well as those that were just finishing their lunches. Pat had returned to the kitchen to take some cookies out of the oven, but I could tell she was still giving Liz, and her story, all her attention.

"A body!" Liz said it so loudly a lady, wearing a dress with pink flamingos on it, turned to look at us.

"A dead body! A dead body down in the basement!" She repeated those last words slowly and clearly, trying to break through the fog of unbelief that enveloped me.

Riverbend is a quiet, respectable little community. Dead bodies just aren't found here, except in Miller's Mortuary. The last time anything exciting happened here was when old man Franklin's car was stolen. Only it turned out it wasn't stolen. He just forgot he'd left it at Walmart, for an oil change.

It's funny how one's mind wanders when it doesn't want to believe something. Like a dead body found somewhere you've just been.

"Em, are you listening to me? Are you daydreaming again?" She raised her voice. "They found a dead body at the Harwood place," she fairly shouted as she leaned towards me. The clatter of teacups and chatter of talk suddenly stopped, and you could hear a pin drop. Now every eye in the tea room was on Liz.

"What did she say?" the ladies were asking each other.

Liz couldn't resist being the center of attention. She stood up and began moving from table to table, telling the news like it was part of the mystery tea parties we periodically held.

"Emily and I were out at the Harwood Mansion this morning on business. We were only there for a few minutes when the Sheriff and some of his deputies came." Liz was good at storytelling and was not above changing a few details to make it more interesting, or to give us a more favorable position. "They came out to protect us, isn't that sweet? Well, anyway, after they escorted us safely home, they searched the whole mansion, and when they got to the basement, they found the body of a dead man."

There were gasps of shock from the ladies and Pat dropped a pan in the kitchen.

Liz shook her head, her red hair bobbing in agreement. "I know, it's shocking, isn't it!" I could tell Liz was enjoying being center stage. "They said there was blood everywhere. The poor man had been stabbed, and he was lying in a huge pool of blood. It had soaked through his clothes, and his hair was all matted."

One lady made a rush for the rest room. Another groaned and held her napkin up to her mouth. She looked pale. There was even a groan from Pat, in the kitchen, at the vivid picture Liz continued to paint.

I stepped to my sister's side. "Enough already," I warned quietly. "You want to drive all the customers away?" I tried to get her to change the subject. "Tell us who he was," I prompted.

But Liz was just getting warmed up to her story. "That's the mystery of it all. No one could recognize him. He'd been dead for so long, his face was all —"I stopped her before she could get too graphic. "Liz, you mean they don't know who he was?" I gave her a threatening look.

"That's right. No one knows who he was, or what he was doing there, at the Harwood place, or who killed him. And to think, Emily and I were there - alone – in that big mansion, with a killer on the loose."

The ladies gasped again. Me, too. The enormity of it was beginning to soak in. We'd been at the mansion. There was a dead body in the basement while we were there. Practically right under our feet. And there was a killer loose in Riverbend. A killer that could have been there, while we were there. Hiding. Waiting...

I could feel the blood draining from my face as my knees turned to jelly. I sank down in one of the fancy tea chairs.

Chapter 4

That night, at the church council meeting, there was more talk about the murder than about church business.

Deacon Dwight Underwood glared at me. "I want to know what you were doing at the mansion in the first place. Apparently, you don't realize the importance of maintaining a respectable reputation as a deaconess. They say you were hauled off to jail like a common crimin-"

Pastor Steve interrupted before Dwight had a chance to finish his accusation. "I don't know where you got your information, Dwight, but Sister Emily has explained the events to me, and she is innocent of any wrong doing."

I don't know why Dwight seemed to dislike me, and resent my being appointed as a Deaconess; except for the fact that I was a woman, and he held strongly to the old fashioned teaching that women should be seen and not heard in church. Oh, we were good enough to teach Sunday School, raise money for missions and keep the church running, but not smart enough to sit on the council. Since I was the church's first and only female Deacon, I got the brunt of his displeasure.

Martha, Pastor's secretary, asked "Do you want that in the minutes?" She attended every council meeting, dutifully taking minutes of the proceedings. I knew she would rather be at her husband's side, who was recuperating from heart surgery, at the hospital.

"Pastor Steve opened a folder and replied, while looking at Dwight, "No, I don't think that personal accusations need to be recorded as part of church business. Now, let's talk about the Easter sunrise service. I assume you're all in favor of the traditional sunrise service?"

I tried to concentrate, but my mind kept wandering back to the mansion. Was it possible that the murderer had been in the building somewhere, hiding, while Liz and I were there? Thank goodness the security alarm had gone off instantly, bringing the police. What if we had discovered the body? Or, worse yet, the murderer?

As if on cue, there was a clap of thunder, and lightning crackled across the night sky. The lights flickered, and we all held our breath. Our local power company is famous for power outages in storms. Another loud clap of thunder, accompanied by a brilliant flash of lightning, did the job. The lights went out.

The battery powered exit sign over the door gave an eerie red glow to the darkened room. Pastor suggested we sit quietly for a few minutes in the hope that the power would return quickly. We waited. I could Hear Deacon Brown, who was sitting next to me, breathe. Someone coughed. After several minutes, Deacon Brown's breathing became slower and heavier. He had fallen asleep. It was not uncommon for the elderly Brown to nod off during council meetings. I just hoped Dwight didn't think it was me, softly snoring!

After what seemed like an eternity to me, Pastor Steve finally suggested we end the meeting. If a transformer had been hit by lightning, it could be hours before a crew got power restored.

I hadn't brought an umbrella and only wore a light jacket. I would get soaked running to the car and would have preferred to wait it out in the shelter of the church meeting room. However, everyone else stood and gathered their things together in preparation to leave. I certainly didn't want to be alone in the building, so I did the same.

The rain was cold and hit hard against my thin hoodie. The wind promptly blew the hood down and I tried to cover my head with a notebook as I made a dash for the car. I was thankful for the remote that unlocked the car door as I ran toward it and scrambled inside.

The streets were dark and empty. The rain was coming down so hard the windshield wipers could hardly keep up with it. I made a mental note to have them replaced. How often is a person supposed to do that? Car maintenance was something I struggled with, without a man in my life to offer advice. The sky lit up with lightning again. I sure wished I had a strong, handsome husband waiting for me at home, on a scary night like this.

I finally reached home and made a frantic run for the front door. The small porch offered little protection from the rain as I fumbled with the door key. The shrubs on either side seemed darker than usual and threatening. Someone could easily hide behind them. But who would wait behind a shrub, in the rain, to attack a tea room proprietor? Before I could answer myself, the door lock gave way to the key and I was in.

I felt a warm touch on my wet ankle, and it moved smoothly across my foot to the other ankle. Crumpet meowed her welcome to me. She didn't like the storm either. I slipped out of my wet hoodie, and picked her up. She was as glad for the company as I was.

"'How's my girl?" I said as I stroked her soft fur. "I know I have candles here somewhere," I assured her, as I felt my way in the darkness to the cupboard. Eureka! Better than a candle, my hand closed upon a flashlight. With the aid of the flashlight, I was able to locate and light several candles. I began to relax.

I checked the front door to make double sure it was locked. Then I put the teakettle on, thankful I had a gas stove. I stumbled my way into the dark bedroom and found my pj's on the back of the door, where I always hung them. They felt warm and safe as I slipped out of my wet clothes and into them. It would be hard falling asleep tonight. The storm was bad enough, but the thought of a man being murdered in Riverbend was overwhelming. Who was he? Why had he been killed? Who was the murderer? Would he strike again? Who would be next?

The lights suddenly came on, filling the room with brightness and chasing the gloom and doom thoughts from my mind.

I made a cup of passion flower tea to relax me, and Crumpet and I settled down on the sofa, with my laptop. I started surfing for matchmaking sites. I wasn't brave enough to register on any of them yet. I wasn't desperate to have a man in my life; it was just times like this that made me feel lonely. I just thought it might be interesting to see who was available. After all, I didn't go to bars or parties, so how was I ever going to meet anyone?

W.D.M. What did that mean? Widowed, desperate, murderer? White, deadly, miserable? Oh, here's the key to the code. "White, Divorced, Male." OK, that's better. The wording went on to say "tall, attractive, likes sports and romantic dinners." So far, so good. "Looking for voluptuous, fun loving, sensual mate." That leaves me out. Another listing read "W.D.M., professional, affluent, nice looking, likes travel and cruises; looking for travel companion." Hmmm, doesn't sound like he wants to travel down the aisle first, though.

I jumped clear out of my skin when the phone rang.

"What are you doing up so late?" It was my sister.

"Answering the phone; why are you calling so late?"

"I just wanted to make sure you were all right. I know how scared you are of thunder and lightning. Did your lights go out, too?"

"I am not scared of thunder and lightning," I lied. "And yes, the power was off here, too."

Liz explained, "I heard a transformer or something was hit over on Elm Street. Marcy's husband, Dave, was called out to fix it. He said there were tree limbs down all over town."

Leave it to Liz to have the latest news or weather report. "Do you want to have breakfast tomorrow morning?" she asked.

"Sure, but it will have to be early." Liz knew breakfast was my favorite meal of the day, and I loved the specials at IHOP. "I want to get an early start on some pinwheel sandwiches for the tearoom tomorrow. But don't drag me out to any deserted mansions again!"

"I've been thinking a lot about that place all day," Liz answered with a sigh. "I wonder if the body has been removed yet, and if they've cleaned up the basement. You know; all that blood and stuff. Sure makes it hard to sell a place with a dead body in the basement."

"Liz, you're not still going to try to sell that monstrosity, are you? Who'd want to buy it now? It's too gruesome."

"But if I could sell it, it would surely earn me the 'Red Feather of Year Award' for the whole state, Emily!" The Red Feather award was a gorgeous ruby and diamond pin, in the shape of a large feather, which the Red Feather Realtors Association wore on their red felt berets. It was an honored and well recognized symbol that they all vied for, male and female alike. But, in all honesty, it looked a lot better on the females. "Anyway, there's something I want to talk to you about."

✳✳✳✳✳

I laid in bed that night listening to the creaks and groans of my old house. The rain had finally stopped, but the wind was still making all the windows rattle. Crumpet was curled up at my feet, as I silently prayed to the Lord. I thanked him for keeping me safe throughout the day, and for blessing me with good health and good family and friends. I thanked him for caring for me according to the scripture "Cast your cares on the Lord, and he will sustain you," (Ps. 55:22 NIV)

I finally drifted off to sleep, wondering what it was that Liz wanted to talk to me about.

Chapter 5

Liz picked me up the next morning, bright and early, and I marveled at how everything looked fresh and vibrant. The world looked bright and clean, freshly laundered by the rain. A large tree limb partially blocked one of the streets, but Liz maneuvered the Ferrari around it. Nothing could deter us from our chosen path this morning – IHOP's breakfast special.

The perky waitress poured us coffee and took our orders.

"It ought to be illegal for anyone to be that cheerful at this hour of the morning," Liz complained.

"You're just not used to being up so early." I sipped the hot coffee, grateful for the effect of caffeine. "Those fancy pinwheel sandwiches take time to make and I like to do them without Pat hanging over my shoulder, giving instructions."

"I don't know how you put up with her." The caffeine was beginning to have its effect on Liz. She studied the menu.

"Well, if I was ever going to see my dream of having a tearoom come true, I had to make the decision that I could get along with her. She had the money. Plus, she had the culinary skills. It works out pretty well, most of the time."

Murder at the Fancy Frills Tea Room

"You still do that 'four things to be grateful for' about her? Name them," she demanded.

I rose to the challenge quickly. "1. She is dependable. 2. She is fantastic in the kitchen. 3. She loves animals. 4. She is neat and clean. Should I go on?"

"No, I can see you've gone over that list so many times you've got it memorized," she grinned.

We placed our order. The perky waitress seemed delighted with our choices. The pancakes soon arrived. I love watching the butter melt over them, running down the sides. I chose boysenberry syrup and drizzled it over them, allowing a puddle of the rich syrup to form on the side of the plate. I would have to skip lunch to make up for the calorie count, but the pancakes were worth it. I savored every forkful.

"Now, what was it you wanted to talk to me about?" I asked in between bites.

Liz stuffed another bite of her blueberry pancake into her mouth. "I showed a condo yesterday to a very interesting man."

I rolled my eyes. Oh no, not again. What would this be; set-up number 36?

"Now, don't give me that look. Your social life is about as exciting as yesterday's coffee." She poured another cup from the coffee pot the waitress had left on our table.

Liz was right about my social life. The tearoom and church work took up most of my time. But I didn't want to admit I needed help finding a date.

"This nice man is moving into town, and setting up a business. Something he does with furniture, and he's a bachelor! Divorced, I think," she explained.

"You think?"

"Well, I asked him what his wife was looking for in a condo, and he said he didn't have a wife, so I'm assuming he's divorced." She paused, fork in mid-air. "He's much too handsome to have been single all his life. Someone would have snatched him up by now. I suppose he could be a widower, though."

"Which condo did you show him?" I hoped I could lead the conversation off in another direction. "Is that one in Bluewater Complex still available?"

She saw right through me. "Don't try to change the subject. What are you doing this afternoon, about two o'clock? He's going to drop by the office to look over some other listings, and if you just happened to be there too, I could introduce you."

"You know how I feel about meeting strangers. I want to know a man is a Christian and has a strong faith and some moral values before I get interested."

"Well, maybe he does – who knows? Just because the last one I introduced you to turned out to be a swindler, doesn't mean they all are." She tried to look repentant.

I mopped up the last bit of syrup with the last piece of pancake. I'd triumphed again in bringing both pancake and syrup to end at the same time. There's nothing worse than a big puddle of syrup left on your plate and no more pancakes.

"No chance," I answered. "It's Marcy's afternoon off, so I'll be at the tearoom all afternoon. We have a large group of Red Hatters coming for lunch. It's always so much fun serving them. The ladies look so pretty in their fancy red hats and purple outfits."

Liz was not one to give up easily. "Well, then I'll just have to bring him in for tea."

"Oh, yes," I couldn't help but laugh. "He'll feel right at home with the red hatters and tea cozies."

We did have a few gentlemen in our clientele, like Pastor Steve and Arthur. Some men would also attend my programs, "Ten Reasons You Should Drink Tea for Your Health." Sometimes a woman's husband would endure a high tea, but mostly our customers were women. "Anyway, we better get going. Those pin wheel sandwiches take time to make," I reminded her.

"You still working out at the fitness center?" Liz eyed me as I slid easily out of the booth. She inched her way across the seat of the booth with some difficulty and hoisted herself to her feet.

"Three times a week, come hail or high water. Four, if I can find the time. When are you going to come for your free trial visit?"

"Yeah, I gotta do that," she reluctantly said. She was about as eager to work out as I was to meet her bachelor find.

✳✳✳✳✳

Pat was already at the shop when I got there. So much for my plan of making sandwiches in peace.

She looked up from the recipe she was studying. "Lousy power company!"

"Good morning to you, too." I could see what kind of morning this was going to be.

"Without refrigeration, the parfait never jelled. I don't trust the custard either. It looks watery, so that's out, too." She didn't bother looking up as she sorted through recipes.

"Don't forget we have those Red Hatters coming for lunch," I gingerly reminded her.

"I know," she growled. 'You just tend to those sandwiches and let me figure out the dessert."

I had the impression there was something more than the loss of refrigeration bothering Pat. She looked more sullen than usual. Even her complaining had lost its verve.

I started cutting the crusts off the bread and rolling it out into a thin layer.

"How's your daughter doing?" I tried to make conversation.

"Trina's the same. It's always money with her."

"Is she still dating that fellow from Westport?"

"You mean that pond scum that calls himself a man?" She closed a cookbook in disgust. "I can't find anything appealing in there. I'll go back to my tried and true Lemon Tarts for dessert."

I could see there'd be no discussion over dessert choices today. Best to keep my mouth shut, and hope she'd get in a better mood soon.

I continued with the sandwiches, spreading the bread with filling, and rolling them up. I wrapped them in plastic wrap to refrigerate for a few hours before slicing.

The rest of the morning progressed smoothly, as I did my best to stay out of Pat's way. Marcy came in to help get things set up for lunch. Pat complained again about the cost of the fresh flowers when Jimmy delivered them. A few early shoppers dropped in for mid-morning scones and tea.

I met the postman when I went outside to see if the flowers in the flower boxes had survived the storm. I sorted through the mail he handed me, and discovered he'd inadvertently included mail for Arthur in my stack of bills and junk mail.

The postman had already moved on down the street, so I decided to deliver Arthur's mail myself. I opened the door; the shop was empty. I called out, but my voice was lost in the clatter of noise coming from the back room. I thought about leaving the mail on the counter, but curiosity overtook me. Isn't that what killed the cat? What was making all that noise?

"Hi," I called out, as I poked my head around the door to his work room. "What on earth are you doing?"

"Emily! How did you get in?" He looked startled and annoyed. Had I interrupted some serious work?

"The door was open. I brought your mail. Is that an old fashioned printing press?" I stared at the big black machine, going clackety-clack.

"Uh, yes. An old antique. I was just playing around with it." He wiped his hands on a towel, and steered me out of the room. Usually, Arthur liked to do a "show and tell" about his antiques, but he surprised me by changing the subject abruptly.

"Did you hear the latest?" Arthur asked as I handed him the mail.

"That depends," I answered. "The latest about what?"

"Someone's going to open a custom furniture factory in the Barkley building."

News traveled fast in a small town. Apparently, Arthur knew all about Liz's new prospect. "And this is good news because?"

"Don't you see? If they are any good at all, I can send all my refinishing and restoring work right to them. I won't have to truck it out of town to be fixed."

"Oh, sure. I see now."

"From what I hear, you might be interested, too." Arthur smiled. "He's single! And he's looking for a place to buy, so he must have money. Here's your chance, honey."

I couldn't believe it. First Liz, and now, Arthur. Was I wearing a sign that said "Single! Needs help?" Or was God preparing me for one of his divine appointments?

Chapter 6

The Red Hat ladies swept into the shop, in all their glory; right on cue, at one o'clock. Their gaiety and chatter filled the tea room. Other shoppers came in to talk to them, and take their pictures. Their "Queen Mother", as she is called, held court in a regal manner, posing and answering questions about the group. She explained to all who asked how they could find information about the Red Hat Society on the internet and how others could form their own chapter. They kept me busy serving and refilling tea cups till midafternoon.

It was almost three before the last of the customers left. Ladies love to linger and gossip till every teapot has been drained and every crumb eaten. Finally, I was able to catch my breath and remember what Liz had said about bringing her new found bachelor into the shop. A glimpse in the back room mirror told me it was time to put on some lip gloss and run a comb through my hair. But before I had time to do that, I heard the door open again and Liz call my name. She sounded alarmed. I rushed out to see what was wrong.

I never saw the dab of lemon curd that someone had dropped on the floor. My heel skidded through it, sending me sailing, like a ship without a rudder, straight into a sturdily built man. Unfortunately, he was bending over at the moment, retrieving a brochure that Liz had dropped. He sprawled head first into a collection of baskets and silk ivy. Gathering momentum, I crashed into the large potted red geranium right next to him. The clay pot cracked into pieces, and dirt and uprooted geraniums covered us both.

Liz broke into gales of laughter. I glared at her, and tried to keep my composure. Then I noticed there was a long piece of ivy draped over the man's left ear. I couldn't stifle the giggle that escaped. He looked at me and laughed out loud. Then he reached over and plucked a geranium stem from my hair.

"You two should see yourselves," Liz howled. "Where's a camera when you need one!" She reached for the man's hand. "Are you all right?"

Oh, fine, leave me sitting here in a pile of dirt, I thought, as I tried to untangle myself from the mess I'd created.

Then a strong pair of arms lifted me out of the debris and onto my feet. "Are you ok?"

"Yes, I'm fine. Are you all right? Anything broken? We carry insurance. Of course, nothing like this has ever happened before, so I don't know how to file a claim. But I'm sure I could call the insurance agent..." I knew I was babbling, but I couldn't seem to stop.

"You're babbling, Emily," Liz confirmed. "Here, let me help you." She brushed potting soil from my shoulders and clothes. "Now that you've met, let me introduce you to Bob Jennings. He's new in town."

I lifted my head and looked into the darkest brown eyes I'd ever seen. They were set in a handsome face, with deep smile lines and little crinkles around his eyes. He had a full head of hair, unusual for a man his age. It was dark brown with touches of grey. He smiled and grabbed my hand in a hearty hand shake. It felt warm, and rough, like a working man's hand.

"Pleased to meet you," his voice was deep, and he smiled as he spoke.

I shook his hand. "It's nice to meet you, too," I smiled back.

"Let me help you pick this stuff up." Liz started to retrieve the baskets and pile them neatly on the shelves again.

"Got a waste basket?" Bob began picking up the pieces of broken pottery.

I ran quickly to the back room, being careful to avoid the lemon curd that had caused the catastrophe. I was glad to see Pat's apron hanging by the back door. She always hung it there when she was finished for the day. I certainly didn't need to be berated by her in front of Liz and Bob. I grabbed the broom and dustpan, as well as the wastebasket.

When we finally had everything cleaned up, I offered to make tea for them.

Bob looked around the deserted room. "Aren't you ready to close?" he asked.

No doubt he was looking for an excuse to get away from me before I created another disaster. And he probably felt like a bull in a china shop with all the feminine frou-frou all about the shop. Me and my fancy frills!

I decided to put the poor man out of his misery. "I understand how you feel. Most men aren't into the afternoon tea thing." I smiled. "It was nice meeting you and I am so sorry I knocked you over."

"Well, you did make quite an impressive entrance," he smiled back. Were those his own dazzling teeth? "Actually, I like tea. My mother used to give tea parties for my three sisters, so I grew up drinking tea."

"Then I'll flip the sign," I said as I turned the "Open for Tea" sign in the window to the "Closed as Can Be" side.

"Anyway, I brought Bob in here on business and we haven't talked business, yet," Liz said as she plopped in a chair at one of the lace covered tables and opened her briefcase.

I could feel his eyes on me as I made the tea and set the table for the three of us. I found a mug for Bob instead of a delicate china cup. I was glad he couldn't see me in the back kitchen as I fumbled setting scones on a pretty plate. My hands felt as if I were wearing boxing gloves, and refused to work gracefully. I couldn't get the lid off a jar of peach preserves and finally resorted to prying it off with pliers from Pat's tool box. In my hurry, I dropped the sugar cubes all over the work bench.

Thank goodness for the partition that blocked the back room work area from the customers view. I was behaving like a silly school girl, falling to pieces just because a handsome man had looked my way. But what if this was the man God had sent in answer to my prayers? *Lord, is this the one? Is he a believer? Lord, give me discernment!*

I took a deep breath, and brought scones and preserves to my two guests. Bob stood, and pulled out the chair for me to sit in.

"Oh, I love these scones," Liz said as she dug into them with gusto. She broke one in half and began slathering it with peach preserves. "Emily's a great cook as well as a business woman."

Liz was being too obvious again in her match making role. I tried to change the subject. "What business are you in, Bob?"

Before he could answer, Liz spoke up. "Bob's in the furniture business. He makes it. I mean, he actually builds beautiful wood pieces, and upholstered furniture, too. He's a real craftsman. You should see the hutch he's working on. It's magnificent." She popped the last of her scone into her mouth.

"It's just a pine country hutch, part of a set. There's a pine split log table, side bench and chairs that go with it. Or, to be more correct, the hutch goes with the table and chairs." He looked down and studied his scone. "Maybe you'd like to see it someday."

I tried not to choke on my scone. "I'd love to!" I blurted out.

"I told Bob that you and Arthur were good friends, and that you'd be glad to put in a good word for him. You know, Arthur could send a lot of business Bob's way, re-finishing and fixing antiques." There was never anything bashful about Liz. Leave it to her to get right to the point.

I smiled, thinking how perfect it was. Arthur wanted someone to send work to, and Bob wanted someone to send him some work. It was just like God to work out details like that. "I'm sure Arthur will be delighted to hear there's someone he can send pieces to locally, instead of sending them out of town."

Then I had a brilliant thought. I could offer to introduce him to Arthur at church and find out if Bob was a church goer or not, at the same time.

"Here's a thought. Arthur and his wife always attend the second service at Riverbend Community Church. I could introduce you to them then, if you haven't settled in at another church yet."

Bob rubbed the back of his neck. "Well, to tell you the truth, it's been awhile since I've been to church anywhere." He paused for what seemed like an eternity. "But I suppose I could come. I'm not much for dressing up and wearing a tie. I'm not even sure if I've unpacked any yet." My heart sank. But then he added, "Is that the church down the street?"

"Yes, right on the corner." I tried to hide my enthusiasm. "The second service starts at 10:30. And don't worry about a tie. You don't have to wear one. We're pretty casual."

"Sounds good. And you'll be there?" He smiled at me, "To introduce us, I mean?"

Was he flirting with me? "I'd be happy to." I felt like jumping up and down, but managed to keep both feet on firm ground.

"I'll be there, too," Liz interjected, "Third row from the back, left side. That's where my husband, Roger, and I always sit. Emily sits up front. She's a lady deacon, you know." I tried to kick her under the table, but missed.

"Oh, really?" Bob looked at me, surprise in his expression. "I didn't know..."

"That there were deaconesses?" I hurried to explain, least he think it was something like being a nun. "Yes, it's not a big deal, just a position of leadership, that's all."

Actually, to me, it was a big deal. I didn't tell him that I was the first female deacon to be appointed and that there was someone on the council that held my every move under a microscope to be sure I did not bring disgrace to the position.

Bob smiled. "Well, all right then. I'll see you at 10:30 at the church. I sure hope the roof doesn't cave in." He looked thoughtful. "Never thought I'd move into a town that is the scene of a murder, open a business and start attending church all in one week."

For a moment, I'd almost forgotten about the murder. Hmmm, a mysterious killer and a new man in town, all in the same week. Was there a connection?

"Have another scone, "Liz said quickly, passing the plate. We all helped ourselves to scones and jam and I refilled the teacups. I was very careful not to spill.

Chapter 7

The next morning I woke early to Crumpet's hungry meow. I decided to take advantage of the wakeup call by getting in some exercise. I pulled on my sweats, filled Crumpet's bowl with her favorite cat food, promised to empty the litter box later, and headed for the fitness center.

I love seeing the sun beginning to peek over the hills in the distance. The morning rays were already promising another beautiful spring day. Tulips and daffodils were showing off their bright colors. The town looked peaceful in the early morning hour; not many folks were stirring yet. It could have been the setting for one of Norman Rockwell's paintings.

The wail of a siren interrupted my pleasant reverie. I hadn't noticed the police car following me. I pulled over immediately, wondering what I had done wrong. Bear climbed out of the patrol car and lumbered over.

"You scared me half to death, Bear. Was I speeding?" I asked.

"Sorry to startle you, Emily. I was hoping you'd see me wave at you, but you never looked in your rear view mirror, and I wanted to talk to you. I just gave the siren one push to get your attention," he apologized.

"Well, it worked. You have my full attention now."

"I thought you'd want to know we got an ID on that body we found out at the Harwood place. Name of Jack Johnson, ever hear of him?" He leaned against the car.

"Well, that's a name as common as John Smith." I thought of all the Johnsons I knew, but I'd never heard of a Jack Johnson. My partner's last name was Johnston, a funny coincidence.

"We're running his prints now," Bear said. "Sheriff says we'll have to contact all the Johnsons in town. Dang, that'll take some work. There must be over a hundred of them just in the phone book." He hitched up his pants. ""Besides that, I have to contact all the merchants in town about the counterfeit money being passed. I'll save myself a trip to your tearoom by warning you right now to be on the lookout for some counterfeit five and tens."

"Really?" I was shocked, "In Riverbend?"

"Yep," he replied. "You know what to look for? Do you know how to spot a counterfeit bill?"

"I don't have a clue," I said. "How do you tell the difference between a real one and a fake?"

"Well," he drawled, "if you handle much money, you can pretty well tell just by the feel of the bill. For instance, if you run your finger over the picture of the President, his clothing has a rougher feel to it than the rest of the bill. It's pretty hard to duplicate the paper that's used for the real bills. And look for red or blue threads that kind of run through the printing. Counterfeiters can't do that, so they try to print colored lines." He leaned into the car window and showed me a five dollar bill. "And the printing might be a little blurry on a fake bill. So far, only fives and tens have been showing up. Just be careful, and if you get anything suspicious, call us right away."

"Thanks for warning me." I hoped I could remember all of his instructions.

He put the money back in his wallet. "You and your sister been breaking into any other houses lately? Sheriff says we better keep an eye on you, since you were the first ones in the house since the murder."

"What? What do you mean? Surely you don't think that we had anything to do with – just because we happened to be – I can't believe you'd think" I sputtered to a stop, the implications of the accusation rendered me speechless. "We were the first ones in the house since the murder?" I asked meekly.

"Seems that way, you didn't see anyone else, did you?" He brushed a doughnut crumb off his shirt.

"We barely got into the place when the security alarm went off. You were there within minutes of the time we entered," I reminded him.

"Well, until we catch the murderer you better be extra careful, Emily. We don't know what kind of a killer we got on our hands. Could be a serial killer, like the Boston Ripper, you know." He straightened up to his full height.

"You mean the Boston Strangler or Jack, the Ripper," I corrected him.

Bear looked puzzled. "No, I think we just got one killer on our hands to worry about, not two."

I decided to let it pass. It was too early to try to untangle Bear's thinking. "I'll be careful." I said. "Can I go now? I want to get some exercise in before I go to work."

Murder at the Fancy Frills Tea Room

Bear waved me on and ambled back to the police car.

The music was beating out exercise rhythm as I opened the door to the fitness center. Terri cheerfully greeted me.

"Good Morning, Sweetie," she grinned.

Funny how we call each other caloric names like Sweetie and Sugar when we're trying to avoid those items in our lives. I started warming up with some stretches. There were several other early risers working out. The dynamic duo, as they were called, were already there. Meg was in her early 70's and her daughter was in her late 40's. Martha was there, too, a look of determination on her face as she worked the ab machine. Betty Sue was there again, an inspiration to us all. She had lost forty pounds and countless inches since joining. I wondered if she was still drink Pu'erh tea, the weight loss tea I'd told her about. My friend, Judy, was also working out, before going to work at the library. I smiled a greeting across the room.

"Did you hear the latest about the murder?" Meg asked me. Before I could answer, she went on. "My husband was down at the coffee shop talking to Sheriff Roy Doyle and he said that Roy said the Coroner's office confirmed the body they found had been killed with a knife."

I nodded, waiting for more.

Meg looked disappointed. Obviously, I was not reacting in the proper manner to her news. "Oh, really!" I finally responded. "Do they know who did it?"

"Not yet. Isn't it awful?" She was getting breathless. It's hard to exercise and talk at the same time when you're 70 and pleasingly plump. "I made Harry check the doors twice last night to be sure they were locked. It's just awful to think a murder could happen here in Riverbend. What's the world coming to?"

"Ever hear of a man by the name of Jack Johnson?" I asked. Meg had lived in Riverbend all her life, and was a walking Who's Who of the town's residents.

"Jack Johnson. Hmmm. There was a Johnnie Johnson. He got married and moved to South Dakota. South Dakota, of all places, can you imagine! Then there's Joe Johnson. He had two sons, Jim and Josh. Let me think, Jack Johnson." She had stopped moving, and was just resting and thinking. "Sounds familiar, somehow. I'll have to think about it. Why do you ask? Is he connected to the murder?"

Judy jogged over to my side and interrupted. "Did I see Liz bring a tall, dark and handsome man into your shop yesterday? Who was that gorgeous hunk?"

Martha overheard her. "A stranger in town? There's a killer here, too, you know. Who was the man you're talking about?"

"Perfectly harmless," I reassured her. But the thought had crossed my mind, too, and gave me an uneasy feeling. "He's opening a new business in town. He bought a condo here, and he's a real gentleman. His name is Bob Jennings."

"Of Jennings Furniture?" a cute young thing in black tights asked.

I hadn't made the connection to the large furniture chain that had gone out of business a few years ago. Was it possible?

"I don't know," I responded. "Maybe. He's going to start building custom furniture and repairing antiques."

"What else do you know about him?" Judy asked.

"He's single." I moved to the next machine.

"Maybe he's a widower 'cause he killed his wife. Maybe he killed her for insurance money, and that's why he has money for a condo and a new business." Cute young thing's imagination was running away with her. Either that or her leotards were so tight they were cutting off oxygen to her brain.

"Or, maybe he's an alien from outer space," I said, trying to make her see how ridiculous her assumptions were. "You've already convicted the poor guy and you haven't even met him."

"I was only kidding, I didn't mean anything," she apologized. "I'm sure he's a very nice guy. Probably even goes to church."

"As a matter of fact, he does," I said proudly. "He's coming to First Community this Sunday." Now why did the thought of seeing Bob again, and in church, bring such joy to my heart? Still, there was this uneasy feeling about him, too.

✳✳✳✳✳

Things did not get better when I got to the tea shop. As soon as I opened the door, Pat stormed out to meet me. "I can't find my pastry cutter. Have you been cleaning up and putting my things away again?"

I closed the door, but left the Closed sign in place. I didn't want any customers coming in while Pat was in such a foul mood. She slammed cupboard doors and banged drawers shut as she searched for her missing utensil.

"Why can't you leave my stuff alone?" The drawer she was searching through fell on the floor. She kicked it under a bench.

"*Lord, help me,*" was all I could pray. "Pat, I haven't seen it. I'll help you look, though."

"I can't do a thing without it. You know it's my lucky piece," she explained. "I used it through my whole tour in Germany."

"I know, I know," I said, looking through the baking pans on the bottom shelf.

"Couldn't sleep all night, and now this," she muttered as she pulled out another drawer.

That's when I noticed how awful she really looked. It wasn't just anger that made her face so red, she also looked drawn and ten years older. Her eyes were red and puffy, too, as if she'd been crying.

"Maybe you'd better sit down and rest and let me look for it," I offered.

"No," she snapped.

Just then my hand felt something underneath an angel food pan. "I found it!" I yelled.

"That's a relief!" She grabbed it out of my hand. "Thanks, Em. Now, get out of my way and let me get some work done in here." She tried to smile.

I gladly moved over to my side of the work room and began the sandwiches. As I began to prepare the fillings, I pondered again how to raise the money to buy Pat's share of the business. I didn't want to ask Liz for it, although she had money to spare and had offered it many times. I felt this was something I had to do on my own. Perhaps it was time to see Phillip Barker at the bank about a small business loan.

The bell above the door jingled at the same time I heard Liz's voice.

"You forgot to flip the Closed sign to Open," she called. "Emily, are you here?"

"Making sandwiches," I called back. "Leave the Closed sign up for a few more minutes."

Liz came bustling back to my work bench. "What's this one?" she asked, dipping a teaspoon into one of the fillings.

"Apricot, turkey, pecan salad," I said, waiting for her reaction to the new sandwich spread.

She smacked her lips in approval. "Mmmm, delish! Sheriff Doyle talk to you yet?"

"No, but Bear pulled me over this morning on my way to the fitness center. He startled me so badly, I almost hit a tree."

"Well, Sheriff Doyle paid me a visit," she said proudly. Liz is not one to be out done. "He thought we might know something about the murder, you know, seen something or somebody, since we were the first ones on the scene. By the way, they found out the name of the guy that was murdered."

"What are you two yakkin' about?" Pat greeted Liz with a nod.

"I'm just telling my sister that the police now know the name of the guy that was murdered." Liz looked up at Pat. You don't look so good. You sick or something?"

"Yeah, Yeah, I'm sick; sick of everything." She turned and went back to her work space. Familiar sounds came from the kitchen, as Pat started her morning routine of baking.

"What a joy she must be to work with every day. I don't know how you put up with her," Liz whispered.

"As a matter of fact, I was just thinking about my finances, and just what it would take to buy her out."

Liz pulled out her check-book from her big purse. "Just tell me how much," she said, pen in hand.

"No, I can't let you do that," I said. "You've helped me out too much already, helping me get into a home of my own. I think I can get a business loan. I've been thinking I should go down to the bank and talk to Phillip."

"Oh, good idea!" Liz beamed. "I'll put in a good word for you. Phillip and I are like this!" she crossed her fingers.

"Yes, I've been meaning to ask you about that. He was so syrupy nice about getting us out of trouble with the police, for breaking into the Harwood mansion. What's going on?"

Liz looked like the cat that swallowed the proverbial canary. And it turned out she did.

"Well, I just happened to run into him and that sweet young secretary of his at the Cambridge Inn over in Westport. And they weren't coming out of the restaurant, if you know what I mean."

"Oh, no," I said, "Poor Helen. Do you think she knows?" Helen was Phillip's wife, a pretty woman herself, who enjoyed playing the role of a bank president's wife. Perhaps that was the problem, it was a role to her, and she loved flaunting her position in the many social clubs she belonged to.

"Phillip tried to avoid me, but I rushed right over to them. They were just coming out of their motel, so it was pretty obvious what was going on. I even made him introduce me to his secretary," Liz grinned shamelessly. "He was so embarrassed at being caught; he could hardly get her name out. He stuttered and stammered and tried to say they were getting some important work done secretly."

"I would have loved to have seen that!" I could just imagine the pompous bank president's red face.

"I reassured him that I'd keep his "work" secret, 'cause that's what friends do for one another. They help one another out. I think he knew what I meant." She paused for a half second. "So, what do you think of Bob?" Liz jumped from one subject to another faster than a tap dancer on steroids.

"He seems nice, but what do you know about him? Is he divorced or a widower? And if he's a widower, how did his wife die? And why does he want to move to a small town like Riverbend?" I guess all the questions asked at the fitness center had me wondering, too.

"I don't know any of that stuff. I just know he's got money, he's single, and he's darn good looking. That's all that's important to me. I think he likes you, too," she added as an afterthought.

"Well, it takes more than good looks and money for me. I want a man who believes in God and —"

I was interrupted by Arthur. He opened the door, and flipped the closed sign to open.

"I'll have a blueberry scone and hot tea to go," he announced. "What do you have to wake me up? I worked late last night and I can't seem to get started this morning."

I suggested English Breakfast tea. The robust, full-bodied tea should do the trick.

"Nice to see you, Arthur," Liz said as I prepared his order. "Have you heard about the custom furniture and upholstery shop that's opening soon? Should be a big help to your antique business."

"Yes, I can hardly wait to meet the guy," Arthur said. "I just got in a wonderful old chair, dating back to the 1700's. It's straight from England. Only problem is, it's in pieces right now. I'm hoping this guy will be the genius to restore it."

"Well, come to second service Sunday, and I'll introduce him to you," I said as I handed him the bag with his breakfast in it.

Arthur paid me, and said "Really? He's a church goer, too? Well, what do you know! I'll be there for sure."

Liz followed him out the door, still talking, and Jean, one of my steady customers, came in.

"Hi, Emily, How are you?

"Fine," I answered. "How are you?"

"I'm getting skinnier and richer every day!" she replied in a rehearsed voice. "Would you like to know how? Come to my meeting tonight and I'll show you how you can **lose** weight and **find** money every day."

Jean believed in network marketing, and had a new product to promote every time I saw her, or so it seemed.

"Sorry, I'm busy tonight," I fibbed. Well, washing my hair counts as being busy, in my book.

"Do you need dessert for your meeting?" I asked, trying to get off the hook.

"Yes, some of those cookies and those," she said pointing at the trays lined up in the display case. "Oh, those look yummy, too."

I packaged them up for her as she reminded me that I could come to any of her weekly meetings, or she would be happy to meet me for a private one-on-one session.

I breathed a sigh of relief as she left. Last month it had been a program to participate in a co-op electric power plan. Her motto then had been, "I'm full of energy and saving money, too." She loved multiple level marketing, and was sure she would make a fortune with it, as soon as she found the right product.

Chapter 8

The remaining days of the week flew by in a flurry of tea parties, appointments and gossip about the murder. Every day Pat looked worse and was more moody than ever. I could hardly wait for my appointment at the bank to see about a business loan. I was relieved to discover that Pat was as anxious to sell her share to me, as I was to buy her out. Maybe a good long rest was what she really needed.

Sunday finally arrived. I had to admit I was acting like a silly school girl about Bob. I found myself daydreaming about him and eagerly looked forward to seeing him in church. Would he really come as he said he would, or was he just being polite and agreeable? I'd know in another few hours.

I showered and dressed in a lavender sheath dress and matching short sleeved jacket. Most of the women in church wore slacks, or even jeans, but since I was a deaconess, I thought it better for me to wear a dress, especially when I assisted in collecting the offering.

Crumpet meowed loudly for her breakfast. I filled her bowl. "Tired of being alone, aren't you? I know that feeling. We all need a little TLC, don't we? When I get back, we'll play, ok girl?" I rubbed her ears and she purred.

Murder at the Fancy Frills Tea Room

When I arrived at church, I scanned the parking lot, but it was too early to expect to see Bob's truck there. "He probably won't even come," I told myself as I entered the church. The musicians were already there, warming up.

Dwight Underwood headed straight for me, a scowl on his face. "Most of the other deacons were here a long time ago. They take their positions seriously."

I glanced around the nearly empty auditorium. The only other deacon there smiled at me from across the room.

"Of course, they probably get to bed earlier than a single woman. Out late again last night, were you?" he sneered.

"No one told me to come earlier than usual today," I replied. "And yes, as a matter of fact, I was out late last night. Why, it must have been at least 8:30 before I finished cleaning at the tea shop."

"Make some coffee for the altar guild," he ordered and turned away.

Somehow I managed to bite my tongue and not say the words that were right there, ready to spill out and cause more damage in our relationship. I began, instead, to think of those four things I could be thankful for, and began to fill the coffee pot.

I finished all my pre-service duties and was seated in my usual seat when the service began. Bob was not there, and I tried to keep my mind on the praise and worship songs that filled the sanctuary. Soon I was lost in the glory of giving praise to the Lord, and as I transferred my thoughts from Bob to the Lord, I was filled with peace once more. I closed my eyes and lifted my hands in praise as I joined the congregation in singing. My reverie was interrupted by the movement of people shifting in their places to make room for a late comer. Why couldn't people be on time?

"Sorry I'm late. I thought you said it started at 10:45" a male voice whispered in my ear.

I opened my eyes and there he was, standing right next to me. Close, our shoulders touching, although mine was several inches lower than his. My heart did a funny flip-flop thing. I hoped my face wasn't turning red, as Liz said it did, when I got flustered.

"Glad you made it," I whispered back.

Pastor Steve gave a good message about finding and knowing the will of God, and then gave a powerful closing. He encouraged people to give their lives to the Lord, and make him the Lord of their lives; to enter into a personal relationship with Jesus Christ, as their Savior. I tried to glance sideways at Bob, wondering how he was responding to all of this. He looked uncomfortable and shifted his weight from one side to another. I think I heard, or maybe just sensed, a sigh of relief when the service was over.

People took their time leaving, chatting with each other as they made their way out the big, oak, double doors of the church. Pastor Steve stood by the door, shaking hands and enquiring about their health, family, job concerns, kids in college, and other everyday concerns. When Bob and I finally got our turn to shake hands, I introduced him to Bob.

They shook hands heartily, and when I told him Bob was opening a custom furniture shop, he got excited. "Great! This town can really use a business like that. I'd love to see your shop, I have an interest in building things, too. Can I drop by one day next week?"

"Yeah, sure, I'm still getting set up, but come on by," Bob replied.

"I like him," Bob said, still smiling as we moved down the steps, "Even if he is a preacher. There's something different about him."

Arthur stood at the bottom of the steps, watching us.

"Bob, there's someone I'd like you to meet. This is Arthur Leeds. He and his wife Sue own the Yesteryears Antique Shop next door to the Tea Room."

"Glad to meet you," Bob extended his hand and engulfed Arthur's hand in a hand shake.

"Not as glad as I am to meet you. Emily tells me you're an expert at restoration and refinishing," Arthur said as he looked at me.

"Well, I don't know about being an expert," Bob laughed. "But I've been known to rescue a few damsels in distress, like Queen Anne and Jenny Lind."

Arthur smiled at the word play. "Well, I've got a whole back room of pieces that need to be rescued," he said. "How soon before you're up and running?"

"Well, things seem to be going faster than I thought they could. I've already found a location, and a condo to live in, so I guess I could be in pretty good shape by the end of next week."

"Great," Arthur said. "I've got a chair that's priceless — but it's in pieces. If you can put it back together again, you'll be a miracle worker."

"Don't know that I believe in miracles," Bob replied. A shadow crossed his countenance. "But bring it by, and I'll see what I can do."

I felt a rough tug on my arm. It was Dwight. "You're needed downstairs." He gave Bob a dirty look, "If you can tear yourself away."

Before I could respond, he turned and stormed off. I knew part of my duties as deaconess was assisting in the counting and recording of the offering, and I intended on doing that as soon as I had fulfilled my promise to Arthur to introduce him to Bob.

Bob and Arthur both looked stunned at the rude interruption. "Forgive him," I explained. "He resents a woman being on the deacon board. But he's right, I do have things to attend to, so please excuse me." I hurried back to the sanctuary to help record the money. Would we have to watch for counterfeit bills?

Bob's voice followed me. "See you later," he called.

Would I really see Bob later, or was that just an expression? Did he mean anything by it? Only time would tell.

*****

Monday morning found me fidgeting in a chair, seated across the desk from Phillip Barker. I clutched several folders of store receipts, bank deposits, etc. The sun cast rays of bright sunshine from the window across the banker's eyeglasses, making it difficult for me to make eye contact with him. He smiled. I felt like snatching his glasses off his nose. "My, that sun is bright," he said, and did me the favor of getting up and pulling the blinds to shade his desk. Was he a mind reader? "Now, what can I do for you?"

I explained my desire to become the sole owner of the tea shop. He kept nodding his head up and down while I presented my case. "Yes, your sister told me you might be coming by," he finally said. He smiled again. It didn't look any better without the sun glinting off his glasses. His eyes belied the smile, looking cold and impersonal. To my surprise, he handed me several papers. "Just fill these out and we'll be glad to set you up with a business loan."

"Don't you want to see my records?" I'd spent hours accumulating them.

"I'm sure everything is in order. Just fill out the loan documents, and we'll take it from there." He stood up as though he was dismissing me.

"Um, how long does it take after I submit them?" I couldn't believe how easy this was going.

"Let's see." He looked at his leather bound day planner. "The loan committee meets a week from Wednesday, so we should have your check drawn about three days after that." He held out his hand for me to shake. I was being dismissed. I couldn't believe it had all been so simple.

"Oh, my goodness. Thank you, thank you!" I was pumping his hand up and down like I was pumping for water. "This is a dream come true. I've wanted this for so long; I never dreamt it could actually happen." I was babbling again.

"Yes, well, have a nice day," he said as he tried to extricate his hand from mine.

I was still pumping for all I was worth. "Oh yes, you've made it a wonderful day." I think he was afraid I might leap across the desk at any moment and embrace him. Actually, the thought did cross my mind.

I walked out of the bank, praising the Lord, and right into Dwight Underwood!

"Watch where you're going, young lady!" Even Dwight Underwood couldn't destroy my good mood. "Oh, excuse me! Isn't it a wonderful day?" I felt like dancing.

"No! Not when I practically get knocked off my feet by someone that can't see straight. Morning hang-over, Emily?" He peered at me, as though expecting to see bloodshot eyes.

"Dwight," I responded, "I don't know where you get the idea that I'm some sort of party animal. I'm a teetotaler, in every sense of the word. Total tea, that's me," I said, as I pointed to the tea room across the street.

"Well, then, that's where you belong. You run your little tea room, and leave the church business to us men," he said sternly.

I'd had enough. "But it's you 'church men' who voted me in, eight to one. It was the general consensus that it was high time for a woman to be on the deacon board, and that word came all the way down from the High Council on the state level. And for your information, I regard it as a great honor, and treat the position with great respect." I felt my face getting hot and knew I was turning red.

"It's only a matter of time before they see how wrong they were," he replied. "They'll see, I know they'll see," he muttered as he continued into the bank.

Murder at the Fancy Frills Tea Room

My thoughts turned once again to finding four things to appreciate about Dwight. It was a real challenge this time. 1. Well, you always knew where you stood with him. He didn't hide his feelings. 2. And he attended church, even though he didn't seem to learn anything from it. Hmmm, it was getting harder. 3. He was consistent. Consistently wrong, but consistent. This was really hard. 4. How about the fact that he didn't spit tobacco! There, I did it. I felt like skipping as I crossed the street to the soon-to-be-mine-alone tea room, but decided that would definitely be un-deaconess like behavior. But, didn't David leap in praise to God? Oh, it was tempting!

I guess it was because I was so wrapped up in my thoughts that I didn't notice the police car pull up to the curb. Not until Sheriff Doyle called my name.

"'Mornin', Emily." He climbed out of the driver's seat.

"Good Morning, Sheriff! Isn't it a beautiful day?" I unlocked the front door to the tea room, thinking Pat must be late today. She usually arrived well before me and left the door unlocked.

He followed me into the shop. "I'm afraid I have some bad news, Emily. You might want to sit down."

The look on his face warned me that indeed, it must be very bad news. I felt my joy and peace go whoosh, like the air out of a balloon.

"We found another dead body, Emily. This time it's someone we all know."

"Liz!" Something had happened to Liz! I felt darkness sweep over me. I'd fainted once before in my life, and felt that same blackness overcoming me. My knees caved in, and I fell into a chair.

A voice was trying to cut through the black fog that engulfed me. "It's not Liz." The voice kept saying. "Liz is alright. Do you hear me?"

I fought my way back to consciousness.

"It's not Liz. Your sister is alright, Emily!" He was shaking my shoulder. "It's not Liz, it's Pat."

Pat. Did he say Pat? "Pat? Pat?" I shook my foggy head. "Pat's dead?" I tried to comprehend what he was saying. "What happened?"

Sheriff Doyle sat down across the little tea table from me. His belly bumped against the table. He looked oddly out of place. I noted that the Sheriff's badge, gun holster and police hat clashed terribly with the pink prim roses. I tried to focus again. The cobwebs started to clear as I comprehended the terrible news.

"We got a call from Westport Police," he explained. A car was found on a rural side road. Turned out it was Pat's car." He paused. "Hate to tell you so bluntly, but there's no other way." He took a breath. "Her body was found in the trunk. She'd been shot."

That black fog was closing in on me again. I tried to focus. Pat shot? Pat murdered! Things like that only happen in the movies. This couldn't be happening. The black fog grew thicker.

"Emily, you alright? Here, put your head down to your knees." I felt a strong hand push my head down.

Finally, the fog lifted and I raised my head. "I'm alright now. I just can't believe it. Who would kill Pat?"

Murder at the Fancy Frills Tea Room

Pat gone. I couldn't get myself to say the word 'dead' yet. It was just beginning to sink in. She had been murdered and she was gone forever.

"You own a gun, Emily?" he asked. "Keep one in the shop for protection?"

"Me? A gun?" I laughed nervously, "No, of course not. I don't like guns."

"Well, had to ask, didn't I?" he said. "Not planning on leaving town or anything are you?"

"Me? No, no, of course not," I stammered. "Where would I go?" Oh, my goodness, the tea room. I'd have to get someone to take Pat's place right away. My mind was a jumble of thoughts.

"Well, we're just starting our investigation." He rose from his chair, preparing to leave. "I just thought you should be one of the first to know. We're trying to contact her daughter, too. Sure hate being the bearer of such bad news."

My thoughts were bouncing around in my head like hail on a tin roof as I walked him to the door and flipped the lock in place. There'd be no tea parties today. I placed the Closed sign in the window. Pat's dead. Who will do the scones? The shop's mine! But I didn't want it to happen like this. Do we have any cookie dough in the refrigerator? Did Pat have a will? Did Pat leave her share of the shop to her daughter? Cancel all reservations for the next few days. When will the funeral be? I should have told her more about Jesus. I wished I had told her how much He loved her.

News travels fast in Riverbend. I'd barely begun to cancel the day's reservations, when I heard a pounding on the front door.

"Emily, let me in," a familiar voice shouted.

I hurried to unlock the door before it fell off its hinges. Liz burst into the room, her red realtor jacket unbuttoned, revealing a red silk blouse worn with matching red pants. Her red beret was tilted at a precarious angle. "Oh, it's terrible. I came as soon as I heard."

I ushered her in. "Horrible," I agreed. "I can't believe it." My knees still felt weak.

"Poor Pat," Liz plopped herself in a chair, out of sight of the front windows. "She was hard to like, but who'd have ever thought…"

I interrupted her. "I know. I feel terrible for her."

"She must have been so scared," Liz shuddered.

"I should have tried harder to witness to her." I thought of all the missed opportunities I'd had.

Liz patted my hand. "Whoever thought Pat would be murdered." Then she added, "I heard she was shot in the head."

Liz always seemed to have an inside track on things.

"How do you know that?" I asked.

Liz opened her compact and began to powder her nose. "Remember that cute little house on Madison Street? The one I sold to that nice young couple from Spring Hill? I cut my commission so they could afford it. Remember? Well, he just happens to work at the County Hospital, and read the Coroner's report, and I just happened to run into him at the coffee shop and...just let's say, we happened to chat about things."

I shook my head in disbelief. "Pat murdered! But why? Who? Who –"

Liz stopped me before I began to sound like an owl. "Lots of suspects, I imagine. Her daughter, for one, or any of the many people she's insulted, sued, or mistreated over the years." She was silent for a moment, then added in a quiet voice, "or you."

"Me?" I wanted to laugh, but it got stuck in my throat and came out more like a croak. "Why me? What are you talking about?"

"Didn't you want the shop all to yourself? Half the town's heard you say that." She dropped the compact back in her purse.

"Sure, but I wouldn't kill for it. You're not serious, are you?"

Liz patted my hand. "Of course, I don't think so. You're my baby sister. I know you couldn't do anything violent if your life depended on it. But you know how people will talk."

As usual, Liz was right. It wasn't long before Sheriff Doyle came to call again. This time he found me at home.

I'd cancelled all the tea party reservations for the next week, closed the shop temporarily, and was nursing a headache one throb short of a full blown migraine. Confusion and anxiety swirled about in the whirlpool that once was my mind.

"Coffee? Tea?" I offered.

"Coffee, black and strong, would be appreciated." Sheriff didn't smile as he said it.

I figured yesterday's coffee would be strong by now, and nuked a cup in the microwave. He declined sugar or creamer.

"Emily, tell me about your relationship with Pat," he sat back in his chair and sipped the strong brew.

"Well, I really don't know too much about her, strange as that sounds," I explained. "Pat was always a very private person, she wasn't one for idle chit chat, you know. " He nodded and I continued, "Seems I've known Pat most of my life, we went to the same school, Pat was a few years ahead of me. But we were in the same Home Ec class. Pat was actually kind of a teacher's aide in my Freshman Home Ec class. I remember, even back then, she was grumpy. If we didn't do something right she'd get upset. She went into the military right after graduation; the Army."

"How'd you two become partners?" he asked, drinking his coffee.

'Cut right to the chase,' I thought. "Well, one day I was down at the gym and Pat was there. She was lifting weights, I remember. I was talking to my friend, Judy, about how my dream in life was to open a tea room and make fancy scones and pastries, but it would probably never happen.

When Judy left, Pat came over and started asking questions. Seems she had overheard my conversation with Judy, and next thing I knew she was offering to go in as a partner. She offered to furnish most of the money, and do all the baking, and I'd be responsible for bookings, advertising, serving – you know, the marketing end of it.

"So she had money?" the Sheriff looked serious.

"She said she'd just gotten out of the military and had been saving all those years. To top it off, she'd just come into an inheritance from a relative."

"And you had your share of money to invest?" He inquired.

"I emptied my bank account, and borrowed a little from Liz; why all the questions, Sheriff?"

He didn't answer my question. "How'd you get along with Pat?"

"Well," I paused. What should I say? Did I need a lawyer? Should I tell him what a tyrant she was to work with? Was I really under suspicion? "Well, I'll admit it wasn't easy working with her. Pat could be pretty difficult to please. She was a perfectionist, you see. It seemed I never could do anything good enough to please her."

"I hear you wanted her out of the picture." He folded his arms over his chest.

A chill went down my spine. It sounded so harsh, the way he put it. "Actually, I was going to buy her out. I was applying for a loan at the bank."

"Oh?" He raised one bushy eyebrow. I always wished I could do that. Raise one eyebrow, that is, not have a bushy one. "Which bank?"

"I talked to Phillip Barker over at Riverbend First National"

A loud knock at the door saved me from any further interrogation. It was Pastor Steve. "Hello, Emily. Sheriff Doyle."

I was relieved when the Sheriff stood and said he was just leaving.

As the door closed behind him, my good friend and Pastor gave me a hug. Pent up feelings of fear, confusion and loneliness were released as tears filled my eyes and ran down my cheeks. "I don't know why I'm crying," I said as I tried to compose myself.

He handed me a tissue, and watched as I tried to calm myself and dried my face. "You've been through a lot, Emily. Your business partner and friend has just been murdered, your livelihood is in trouble, and your reputation is being questioned."

He said that last part with hesitation.

"What do you mean?" I asked, dreading the answer. Was it all over town that I was a suspect?

"I'm afraid Dwight Underwood is having a field day implying all sorts of things about you. So, when I saw the Sheriff's car in front of your house, I thought I'd better stop by to make sure you weren't under arrest or anything."

"You don't think I had anything to do with Pat's death, do you?" I trembled, waiting for his answer

"Of course not! Emily, I know you too well to even think that for one second. But people will be people, I'm afraid, and they love a bit of gossip." We sat down on the sofa.

"What is everyone saying?" I had to know, even though I didn't want to know.

"Well, not everyone of, course. But, some are implying that you and Pat never got along. They heard arguments. And they say you wanted the shop all to yourself." He looked away.

"That's true, I did." I got up and retrieved the loan papers from my desk. "I was applying for a bank loan to buy her out."

"And Pat was going to sell her share of the business to you?" He glanced through the loan papers.

"Yes, she had agreed. She hadn't been feeling well for some time. She seemed more depressed than usual, and said she was ready for a change. She wanted to get away for a while. But the loan wasn't final yet."

"Well, let's think about this. Is there anyone else who would benefit from Pat's death? Besides you? Or anyone who would have a reason to kill Pat?" He took out a notepad and pen from his pocket.

"She doesn't have any friends that I know of; just her daughter, Trina. They weren't close. Pat complained about Trina borrowing money all the time. But then, she complained about everything. She didn't like Trina's friends, especially her boyfriend."

"Did Pat have a husband?" he asked.

"She said her husband had died a long time ago. She never talked about him, except to complain about him," I answered. "It sounded like they might have been separated when he died."

"So, we have a woman with more enemies than friends, a daughter in need of money, and not much more to go on. Did Pat have money of her own?" His pen was poised, waiting for my answer.

His sudden change of thought surprised me. "She had savings and she had inherited some money a few years ago from an Aunt. That's why she had money to put into the tea room. I don't know how much she inherited though."

"And there's one other thing to take into consideration," he said thoughtfully. "No, maybe two."

"What's that?" I asked.

"Pat's murder isn't the only one. There was a body found out at the Harwood place, remember? Maybe there's a connection between the two."

"You said there were two other things?" I wondered what the second fact was.

"I don't even like to consider the next one. Not at all. But all of this has happened since Bob Jennings came to town. It might just be a coincidence. I certainly hope so, but it is something to take into consideration." He added Bob's name to his list.

Pastor Steve then did what he does best. He prayed, *"Father, we thank you that we can bring all things to you. We thank you that nothing is too difficult for you. We thank you that you are the God of all peace and understanding. Father, we pray for truth and light to come into this situation. We ask that you would divinely intervene in this situation, and bring to justice the one responsible for these crimes. We ask that you would comfort Emily, and give her divine peace that passes all understanding, and give her direction and guidance in all the decisions she must make. Help her to hear from you and know that she is not alone. We ask that you would be glorified in this and every situation. In Jesus name we pray."*

Chapter 9

I opened the door to the fitness center and was greeted by a blast of fast music. Several 'regulars' as well as a few new faces were working out with vigor. I smiled and waved a generic hello to everyone, and made my way to a machine. That's when I noticed it. Conversation had stopped and no one was making eye contact with me. My good friend, Terri, was not at the front desk. Terri was the manager and practically lived at the center, but today Candy was running the desk. She was on the phone when I entered. She finally hung up, and looked up at me.

Before she could look away, I spoke up. "Hi, Candy. What's new?"

Candy glanced around the room. "You tell us. When is Pat's funeral? How's the police investigation going? Any suspects? When are you going to open the tea room again?"

Now every eye was on me, waiting for my answers. I tried to remain calm under that barrage of questions. "I understand Pat's daughter, Trina, wants a simple service just as soon as the Coroner releases Pat's body. Probably next week."

"I didn't know there was a daughter," said one of the dynamic duo.

Murder at the Fancy Frills Tea Room

"Yes, she lives over in Westport," I explained.

"Can't picture Pat as the motherly type," said a woman in a pink jogging suit.

"Be careful how you talk about the dead," said the woman working out next to her.

"It's just so awful!" said another. "Two murders in less than two weeks. Makes you wonder who's next."

"I wonder more who the killer is," said Candy. She turned to me. "I hear the police have a suspect."

Before I could start to defend myself, the pink jogging suit lady spoke up. "I heard that, too; some guy that's opening a business here in town. Nobody seems to know much about him, but he showed up the same week they found that body out at the mansion." I lost my rhythm for a moment and almost fell off the machine I was exercising on, at the thought of Bob being a suspect.

I was glad to see Judy come through the door. She came right over to where I was working out. "Emily, I'm so glad to see you. How are you holding up through all this? It must be terrible for you. Pat was your partner, and to think she's been murdered!"

I appreciated her true concern. "I'm doing the best I can," I said.

"What about the tearoom?" she asked.

"It's closed for now. Till after the funeral, anyway," I said.

"How will you manage without Pat?" She took her place on the machine next to mine.

"I guess I'll have to hire someone," I said. "I can do most of the things Pat did, and hire someone to help with the rest."

"You can bake?" Judy looked surprised.

"Sure," I said, with a confidence I didn't really have. "I was planning on buying Pat out one day anyway, and so I was prepared to take over the kitchen."

"Well, now you won't have to buy her out," the lady in pink smiled knowingly. A few others exchanged glances.

Judy broke the silence. "Emily, if there's anything I can do to help..."

"Pray," I said. "Pray the killer is brought to justice, and pray for Trina, Pat's daughter. I don't think there is any other family."

"I wonder why Pat was killed," the lady in pink mused.

"I don't know, but it looks like I'm going to have to find out a few things about Pat's murder in order to clear myself." I glared at the lady in pink. She looked away.

*****

The more I thought about it, the more it seemed the right thing to do. I was clearly under suspicion, by the whole town as well as the police. That night, I sat down with Crumpet in my lap. I took out a notebook and pen and proceeded to write down all I knew about the murders. It didn't take long. For all the time I'd worked with Pat in the kitchen, I really didn't know much about her. She'd been in the military, and had a daughter. What did I know about the other murder, the one at the mansion? Was there any connection? And were there any suspects? Besides me?

Murder at the Fancy Frills Tea Room

Oh yes, there was Bob. What a lovely thing to have in common with a man you are interested in. Both of us suspected of murder!

I jumped when the phone rang, sending Crumpet flying out of my lap. To my surprise, it was Trina, telling me the Coroner's office had released her mother's body, and the funeral was set for Friday. There were so many questions I wanted to ask her, but it hardly seemed appropriate to play twenty questions now. But it seemed Trina wanted to talk.

"We were never really close, you know, but-" her voice broke.

"I know," I said, not sure that I really did.

"I always hoped we'd – but she never- she wasn't a happy person, was she?" She choked back a sob.

"She seemed happiest when she was working," I said truthfully. "She loved to bake."

"She liked you, you know," she said.

I was surprised to hear that. "I'm sure your mother loved you," I said.

"Did she ever talk about me? Complain?" There was a sniffle.

"Well, you know your mom; she was a private person. She never talked about anything personal." I decided to press on. "Trina, do you know if she had any enemies?"

"No. She didn't have any friends, but I don't' think she had any real enemies either."

Was Trina sincere in her grief or was it just an act? I hung up and returned to my notebook. Under suspects I penciled in Trina's name. She probably was the sole beneficiary of Pat's will, if there was one.

The next morning I called on Pastor Steve in his office at the church. I wondered how Martha, his secretary, would act towards me. Martha had been at the church longer than the Pastor. Surely she'd heard the gossip about me.

I should have known better than to doubt her character. Martha turned away from her computer as soon as she saw me and came around her desk to give me a big hug. "Emily, it's so good to see you. How are you doing, dear?"

"Actually, I'm not sure. Sometimes it seems like the whole world has caved in on me, and sometimes I feel the Lord strengthening me and telling me everything will be alright. I'm afraid my faith isn't as strong as I'd like it to be," I admitted.

"Now, don't you be thinking that way, young lady. There's nothing wrong with your faith. You feel God is strengthening you; that's good. But, that ol' Satan doesn't like that, so he's the one who brings doubts and fears to your mind. Just don't listen to him, honey. You just claim God's promises, right out loud, and just watch that old enemy flee." She held me tight against her ample bosom in a comforting bear hug.

There was as much ministry that went on in the church office as there was in the Pastor's office, thanks to Martha's love and wisdom. Many a tear had been shed on her shoulder, and I could feel the tears welling up in my eyes.

"Thanks. I'll remember that." I released myself from her arms and reached for a Kleenex on her desk. "Do you think Pastor Steve has time to see me?"

"I always have time for you, Emily. Come right in." Pastor Steve stood in the doorway.

I dabbed my eyes, gave Martha a smile, and found a chair in Steve's office. I liked his small office. The walls were covered with bookshelves filled with books, colorful trinkets and mementos of his love for foreign missions. Several framed cartoons hung on the wall behind his desk, right along with his theology degrees and certificates of ministerial accomplishments. A small American flag was nestled in a desk holder.

"What can I do for you, Emily?"

"I'm not sure," I told him frankly. "I feel I need to try to do something...I want to find out..." What did I want to do? I didn't know anything about investigating a murder. "I need help." I finally blurted out.

"That's what I'm here for," Pastor Steve said calmly.

"They think I killed Pat, so I'd have the tea room all to myself. Somehow I've got to prove my innocence, but I don't know how to do that. So, maybe if I can find out more about Pat, I could discover who else would want her dead." I was explaining it to myself as well as to Pastor Steve.

"All right," Pastor Steve said. "I understand what you're thinking, but don't you think you should leave it up to the police?"

"But they think I did it! They might not look any further. The only other suspicious person in their mind is Bob

Jennings. But why would he want to kill Pat?" The Kleenex was now nothing but shreds in my hands.

"I see." Pastor Steve looked thoughtful. "Not much experience in solving murder mysteries in this county, is there? And with the elections coming up in a few months, the Sheriff will want to have this all tied up in a neat little package. The sheriff can't afford to have an unsolved mystery hanging over the voting booths."

A new shiver of fear ran down my spine. "I hadn't thought of that. What can I do?"

"Well, I have to go over to the county jail this afternoon for my weekly chaplain visit." Pastor Steve looked thoughtful. "I can stop at the courthouse and check on records. Marriage, divorce, birth records are all there and that should tell us a few things about Pat. And, since I'm doing the funeral in a few days, I'm in a good position to talk to Trina. I'll find out as much about her mother as I can."

"Oh, that would be a big help," I said. "I'm surprised you're doing the funeral service. How did that come about?"

"I'm surprised, too. I know I wasn't one of Pat's favorite people, if she had any." He smiled. "But Trina called me, and so of course, I said I'd be glad to help. She said she knew her mother didn't attend church, but she had seen me in your shop, so I was the first one she thought of."

"I wonder what the police have found out about the other murder; the Johnson man. I'll see what I can find out about that, too," he continued. "Then, there's Bob Jennings." Pastor tapped a pencil on his desk. "Somehow, I don't see him as a dangerous character. It was nice seeing him in church and meeting him afterward. I liked him. But, we don't know much about him. Why don't you see what you can find out about Bob? Does Liz know him well?"

"Liz knows a little about everything and a lot about nothing," I grinned, "Except real estate. She could sell an igloo to a Hawaiian. And she'll need all her talents to sell that old Harwood place. The place is so run down and gloomy, and now it has a murder to add to its history."

✲✲✲✲✲

With that in mind, don't ask me why I found myself driving down the long, winding road to the deserted mansion. It seemed to draw me there like a magnet. It pulled me along the neglected gravel road. Once, it had been a road covered with carefully placed pristine white gravel. Beautiful flowering shrubs and bushes had ushered celebrities and politicians in chauffeur driven limos down the road to the famous mansion. Now, overgrown shrubs and bushes clawed the edge of the road, fighting for dominion.

I parked the car at the entrance of the front circular driveway. The mansion, once called the Queen of Architectural Beauty, now looked like an ugly hag waiting for Halloween. The front porch sagged and some of the porch railings and pillars were missing. The paint was peeling and there were bricks on the ground that had fallen from the chimneys.

I got out of the car, pulling my lightweight jacket around me. A brisk, cold wind tugged at me. It was beginning to look like rain. Don't ask me what I was looking for, I certainly didn't plan on trying to get into the mansion. You couldn't have paid me to do that, even if I found an entrance. I walked along the path leading to the front door and around the side of the house. The window that Liz had broken, on our earlier visit, had been boarded up again.

A gust of wind blew my scarf right off my neck. Luckily, it got snagged on one of the bushy shrubs near the path. I bent down to retrieve it, and something shiny caught my eye. There was a button, almost buried, in dead leaves. It was still shiny and new looking. That meant it hadn't been exposed to the weather for very long. The gust of wind that had snatched my scarf apparently had blown away the leaves that had hidden the button from the police when they were searching for clues. Or, perhaps they just hadn't searched very well.

"Hello! What are you doing here?" It was a man's voice.

I just about jumped right out of my Hanes undies. I looked up, right into the surprised eyes of Bob Jennings.

"I'm not sure...I just thought..," I slipped the button into my pocket and untangled my scarf from the bush. "The wind blew my scarf..," I hate it when I babble. I took a deep breath. "What are you doing out here?"

"I've heard so much about this place, I had to come and take a look for myself. What a shame to see this place going to ruin. There's still a lot of good lumber in this old beauty. It could still be saved." His gaze swept across the front of the building, and I could almost see the restoration going on in his mind. Then he turned to me. "So, what brings you out here?"

We walked around the building together. "I don't know exactly. I was talking to Pastor Steve about it, and I just had a strong desire to come out and look around the grounds. It's such a famous place, you know."

"I've heard a lot about it. Built back in the days before prohibition, wasn't it?" he asked.

I nodded. "The story is that Oliver Harwood made his fortune in fur trading, and then married a rich heiress from the East coast. Together, they built quite an empire. Their children went on to be even more successful. After a few generations, Harold Harwood lost it all in the stock market. The mansion was sold several times, and then ended up in the hands of a notorious gangster. They say he was connected to the mafia. When he was killed, it sat empty for several years. Nobody seemed to want it. Now look at it."

"Abandoned. Deserted. The perfect place for a murder," he said quietly.

The sky had turned dark with storm clouds, and the mansion looked like the setting for a Hollywood horror movie. I looked at Bob. I must be out of my mind. Here I am, in the perfect place for a murder, with a man some people suspect of murder! I looked away quickly, before he could read my mind. Was he capable of such a thing? "*Lord, give me discernment,*" I silently prayed. "*And protection,*" I added. Just in case.

"You mentioned talking with Pastor Steve." I was glad Bob changed the subject.

"Yes, stopped in to see him this morning. It seems I'm one of the suspects in Pat's death, and I needed to ask Pastor Steve for some help."

"Knocking off your partner, 'cause you wanted the business all for yourself," he grinned at me. "Yeah, you look like the dangerous kind. I should be scared, out here all alone with you. I might be attacked with a tea bag at any moment."

I had to laugh at the absurdity of it. "Two murder suspects, each suspecting the other!"

"What do you mean – two suspects?" He stopped walking and looked at me in disbelief.

"Didn't you know? There's a suspicious man in town. He arrived just about the same time a dead body was found – right here in the basement of this place. No one knows anything about him, and then suddenly there's another dead body found. Looks bad for the new guy with all the money." I raised my eyebrows, wishing I could raise just one, like the Sheriff.

"Oh, I see. So, that's why I've been getting the third degree from everyone I meet. I thought people were just being nosy." He kicked a fallen branch out of the way.

I pulled my jacket closer around me as the wind tugged at it. "It's election year, and I'm really afraid the Sheriff is going to hang this on anyone he can. And you and I, my friend, are looking like the easy way to win an election!"

Before Bob had a chance to answer, the threatening storm clouds broke loose, pelting big, cold drops of rain down on us.

"My car's round back," Bob shouted over a clap of thunder.

"Mine's in front," I called back. We both ran for our cars.

He followed me out on the gravel road, back to town. My windshield wipers could hardly keep up with the rain. I pondered our conversation, and wondered if Bob wanted to continue it. Should I drive home? Would he follow me there? Did I want him to? I remembered the dishes in the sink and the smelly cat litter. Liz. I could drive to Liz's office. It would be a good place to talk, providing he followed me there.

I parked in front of her office, but he continued down the street. I sighed. Relief was mixed with disappointment. I wanted to spend more time with him, to know him better. A lot better. He was the first man I'd been attracted to in ages. I was sure he had nothing to do with the two murders. It was just a coincidence that he arrived just before they occurred. And just a coincidence that he was at the old mansion today. Wasn't it?

I made a dash for Liz's office. My muddy shoes squished as I made my way to her desk. I brushed my wet hair out of my eyes, and tried to look dignified as I passed other realtors showing listing photos to prospects.

"Look at you!" Liz hooted. "Where have you been? Don't you have enough sense to come in out of the rain?"

"I did come in. That's why I'm here," I said as I plunked down in an upholstered arm chair.

"Watch the mud, dearie," she said, and handed me some paper towels.

I dried my face first, and then went to work on the shoes.

"You're just in time for lunch," she said. "I ordered in today. I could see that storm brewing, and I didn't want to get caught in it. Unlike some people, I plan ahead!" She unwrapped a big sandwich. "Want half? It's turkey on whole wheat, with avocado. I've also got potato salad, chips, and cookies, all from Max's deli."

"Mmm, that sounds good." I was suddenly hungry and cold.

"You shivering? Here, have some coffee." She opened a large container of coffee, marked hazelnut, and poured some into a cup. She offered the container, still three fourths full, to me.

I savored the rich flavor and let the hot brew warm my body. I cupped my hands around the Styrofoam container, enjoying its warmth. Liz proceeded to divide potato salad, chips and cookies on a paper plate, with the half sandwich, and handed it to me.

"So, tell me, where have you been?" she asked as she bit into her sandwich.

"Out to the Harwood place."

She dropped her pickle. "What on earth for?"

"I don't know. I just wanted to look around. Just outside, of course. And you wouldn't guess who else was there."

"Oh, no. Sheriff Doyle caught you nosing around again?"

I shook my head. "No. Bob Jennings."

Liz almost choked on the sip of coffee she had just taken. "Really? What was he doing there?"

"Same thing I was. Just looking around. He said he'd heard so much about the place, he wanted to see it for himself."

"Hmmm. Guess that makes sense. Then what happened?" She retrieved her pickle.

"Then it rained, and I got wet."

"Come on, there has to be more than that. Weren't you scared of him, being alone in that deserted place?"

"No more than he was of me. I could be a dangerous killer, remember?" I bit into the sandwich.

"He actually heard that about you? He told you he heard that?" She stopped eating.

"Yes, and I told him what the town gossip was about him."

"He didn't know? Then what happened?" Liz leaned forward in anticipation.

"Then it rained, and I got wet." I was enjoying this.

"He didn't defend himself? Tell you anything?"

"No, not really. I explained to him that Sheriff Doyle was anxious to find someone to pin the murders on, and either one of us would do just fine, as long as it was before election time. Then it rained and I got wet."

"That's it?" She looked disappointed.

"The storm broke loose, and we both ran for our cars," I explained.

"Did he say he'd call you or anything?" Liz was a romantic at heart.

"I think he wanted to talk more. I sure did," I admitted. "He followed me out of the property, and I was hoping he'd follow me to talk more. But I didn't know where to go. I didn't want to take him to my messy house, so I came here."

"I see." She munched her cookie thoughtfully. "Maybe the two suspects will have to help each other clear their names."

"My thoughts, exactly." I drank my coffee as I thought more about it.

✳✳✳✳✳

The day for Pat's funeral was a busy one. I woke feeling fat and sluggish. I hadn't taken time to exercise for three days, and I'd been eating all the wrong stuff. So I pulled on my sweats and headed for the gym. I got there before the usual crowd, so I was able to concentrate on my work out and do some heavy praying and thinking as I moved from one machine to another.

"Lord, I commit this day to you, and I praise you and thank you for this beautiful day you've given me. It's like a clean slate, just waiting for you to write instructions on it. Lord, please help me to clear my name in this awful mess, and Bob's name, too.

Only you know who's committed these terrible crimes. Please bring them to justice. And Lord, if Bob's the right one for me, please, make it clear and bless our relationship. But, if he's not the right one, help me to see that, and let this interest I have in him just fade away. 'Cause I'd rather be right with you, Lord, than wrong with anybody else. Amen."

✳✳✳✳✳

Exercise wasn't the only thing I'd been neglecting. My house was a mess. The funeral wasn't till three in the afternoon, so I stacked the dirty dishes in the dishwasher and set it humming. Once the counters were cleaned off I dealt with the accumulated mail overflowing on the snack bar. I tackled the kitchen floor with a mop next. A clean kitchen always makes me feel better. My adrenalin must have still been pumping from my work out, 'cause I dusted and vacuumed the whole house. Granted, it's a small house, but I still felt like the Queen of Clean when I was finished.

I skipped lunch and busied myself with tea house business next. I set a date for re-opening, and began ordering supplies, placing advertisements in the weekly newspapers, and re-booked Red Hat luncheons. I even set an appointment to interview people for kitchen help. Bless that employment agency!

It was after two when I headed for the shower. My blonde hair co-operated with the blow dryer for a change, and didn't need many touches with the curling iron. I didn't want to wear too much make up, but I still wanted to look nice. I chose a subdued rose for lipstick and blush, and went easy on the eye makeup. I dressed in a navy blue suit and was satisfied with the image in the mirror.

When I arrived at the church, many were already there for the funeral. Curiosity seekers mainly, not many familiar faces. Liz beckoned to me from her seat in the fourth row from the back. She was wearing a deep purple plaid pant suit with purple open toed shoes. Purple painted toe nails peeked out from her Gucci's. "Never thought Pat knew so many people," she whispered.

"Curiosity seekers," I whispered back.

"Whose speakers?" she asked.

"Curiosity seekers," I said louder.

A woman in a straw hat turned around and glared at me.

I surveyed the room. Trina sat close to the front. She was wearing a black dress, black hat and sat up straight. She was alone. She often turned to glance around, as if she were watching for someone. Then her eyes made contact with someone, and I turned to see who it was. The man that had been with her at the tea shop, arguing with Pat, moved toward her. His long black hair was combed straight back and tied in a ponytail. His face and hands seemed pale in comparison to his dark beard and mustache. He wore khaki cotton pants, and a poor fitting tweed jacket.

He made his way down the aisle and sat next to Trina and took her hand. They whispered a few things to each other.

"Her boyfriend?" Liz whispered.

"Looks like. Pat didn't like him. Called him pond scum," I whispered back.

"Ron Some?" I was beginning to think Liz needed a hearing aid.

"Pond scum," I whispered louder.

The woman in the straw hat stood up. She gave me a dirty look and moved to another seat.

I hoped Dwight Underwood wasn't within hearing distance. He'd accuse me of calling parishioners curiosity seekers and pond scum!

During the musical interlude provided by Hattie Blumgarten, Sheriff Doyle quietly came in and took a seat in the last row, normally reserved for ushers.

Pastor Steve gave a lovely service. When he asked if there was anyone who wished to say something about Pat, no one moved. Liz nudged me. I looked at her blankly. She elbowed me again while looking straight ahead. I looked down, examining my hands in my lap.

"Say something," she elbowed me again.

It looked like no one was going to say anything in Pat's behalf. It was up to me. I gulped and rose to my feet. That's when I saw him. Bob was sitting two rows in back of me. He gave me a little smile of encouragement, and a slight nod.

I made my way to the microphone, not having a clue as to what to say. *"Lord, please don't let me babble. Fill my mouth with the right words."* My mouth felt like Crumpet had been sleeping in it.

"Pat was a very interesting person," I began. Trina gave me her full attention. She looked as if she expected to learn something new about her Mother. I couldn't let her down.

"Uh, I found I could always depend on Pat. She was a consistent person." *I could depend on her to be consistently difficult.* "She had a different way of looking at things." *A negative way.* "As many of you know, Pat and I were partners at the Fancy Frills Tea Room." *May as well get in a little advertisement.* "In fact, without Pat there probably wouldn't be a Tearoom." *True enough, she had provided most of the money.* "Pat was a hard worker, and a wonderful cook." I was beginning to warm up to speaking into a microphone. I kind of liked the sound of my voice, amplified. "She served in the Army and cooked in some of the best kitchens in Europe." There was a slight murmur of appreciation at my touch of humor. With a little more encouragement like that, I might turn into a stand-up comedian! "Pat made the best scones and the best Quiche Lorrain in the state of Wisconsin." Liz was frowning at me.

"She was an important person to me, and I shall miss her. I can't imagine why anyone would have...I mean, it's hard to understand why..." Was it proper to use the word "murdered" at a funeral service? What could I say to get myself out of this? "She loved her nation and her daughter, Trina, and uh, um, other family members and friends." I didn't know what else to say, so I gave the microphone back to Pastor Steve. No one else went forward to say anything.

The service concluded after Hattie sang "Onward, Christian Soldiers." We all marched out of the sanctuary over to the fellowship hall. Bob fell into step beside me and Liz. "You did good," he said.

"I thought she was going to give the whole tearoom menu," Liz said.

Bob laughed. I liked the way the crinkles formed around his eyes when he laughed. "You did just fine," he smiled down at me.

We helped ourselves to coffee and cake provided by the Helping Hands Women's Ministry of the church. I remembered I hadn't eaten lunch and the thin slice of white cake only made me hungrier. Liz helped herself to two more, but I didn't want Bob to think I was a glutton. I remained hungry. Pastor Steve joined our table.

"I see you're working on our little project," he said as he pulled out a chair.

"Oh, that – yes, I mean no, not really. Well, sort of. " I was babbling again. "How about you?"

"Emily and I are trying to find out a little more about Pat's background and who might have wanted to see her dead," he explained to Bob and Liz, who were looking at us with questions in their eyes.

Murder at the Fancy Frills Tea Room

"What have you found out so far?" Liz leaned forward.

"Well, Pat was married to a Jack Johnson. His name is on Trina's birth certificate as the father. They were divorced a year later.

"But Pat's last name was Johnston," I reminded him. "It was spelled differently."

"She just added the 't'. Sheriff Doyle said as he stepped forward and sat down at our table. "I could have saved you a lot of trouble if you'd stopped by and asked," he said to Pastor Steve.

"You mean the murdered man out at the Harwood Place was Pat's ex-husband?" I was stunned.

"That's right, Emily. Ex-husband and ex-con," the sheriff continued to stun us.

"No wonder she never talked about him. I always thought Trina's father was dead," I muttered.

"That's what Pat wanted people to think. Especially her daughter," he explained.

"Can you tell us why he was serving time?" Pastor Steve asked.

"Had quite a record, actually. Fraud, bad checks and counterfeiting. That's what got him into the big time, and into prison." The Sheriff looked around the room.

"Whew," Bob exclaimed. "So, first Pat's ex shows up, dead, and then Pat. How do you suppose that all ties together?"

"Don't know." Sheriff Doyle leaned back and took a deep drink of coffee, "Yet."

"Maybe he got out of jail, saw the teahouse as a money maker and wanted in on it; wanted to claim half of Pat's partnership." He looked directly at me as he spoke.

I choked on my coffee. "That's ridiculous. The tea room is hardly a money maker. We barely turn a profit. Besides, Pat wouldn't leave it to him. She told everyone he was dead."

We were starting to attract attention. Pastor Steve put his hand on mine. "I'm sure Sheriff Doyle wasn't implying anything, Emily."

"There must be a reasonable connection to the two murders," Bob said, "and we'll find it."

"That's another thing," Sheriff Doyle said as he stood up. "What were you two doing out at the Harwood place the other day?"

"Just looking around," Bob answered before I could speak.

"Find anything?" the Sheriff asked.

I remembered the button, and was almost going to speak up, just to show him his investigation wasn't very thorough. You know how sometimes you hear that still, small voice in your head warning you? That's what I heard just then, saying not to tell them about the button. Not then, not yet. I shook my head.

"Well, just leave the investigations to us. We don't need any help from you two," he warned as he moved away.

Trina sat at the next table, alone with her boyfriend. They had been listening. She was sniffling. He looked uncomfortable.

Pastor Steve rose to join them, and we all followed. "Sorry you had to hear it that way," he said to Trina.

"I never knew...I always thought he had died when I was a baby. I never knew...Oh, how awful," she cried into her hankie, "my father, a common criminal!"

"I never knew, either," I consoled her. "The few times Pat ever talked about him, she used the past tense, so I assumed he had died a long time ago."

Pond Scum's jacket had seen better days, now that I could see it up close. The stitching around the breast pocket was torn loose. His hair was slicked back with heavy oil or gel. I didn't want to touch him, but I did want to be introduced to him. I stuck out my hand and said, "I'm Emily Millerton."

He looked surprised. "Sammy Torman," he answered. He shook my hand and I fought the urge to run to the nearest rest room to wash my hands

"You live here in town?" I was surprised at Bob's question.

"Sammy's my friend," Trina intervened. "He lives over in Westport. He, uh, he's new in the area."

"Oh, where did you live before that?" Bob grilled him.

"Uh, Madison."

"Oh, yeah? I know that area a little. Do any fishing on Lake Michigan?" Bob smiled as he spoke.

"Uh, no, never had time." He turned to Trina. "I gotta go."

"Oh, but..." she saw the look he gave her and agreed. "I'll go now, too."

"Now, that's a suspicious character, if I ever saw one," Bob said as he watched them go.

"Love must be blind," I said in Trina's defense. "What was all that about fishing?"

"Just doing a little fishing of my own," Bob smiled. "There's a lot of fishing done in Madison, but it's not on Lake Michigan. It's Lake Mendota. Madison isn't anywhere near Lake Michigan. If he'd really lived there, he'd know that."

"A little detective work, hmmm?" Liz gave him a quizzical look.

"A detective that needs detecting himself, is that what you're thinking, Liz?"

I hoped I didn't look as guilty as I felt. It's exactly what I was thinking.

"Let me save you ladies some time and effort. I lived in Madison for the past twenty-five years, where I ran my own furniture factory. I was a member in good standing of the Better Business Bureau. Feel free to check me out. I was married, and have two sons, both grown and on their own. My wife, Carol, died two years ago." He became silent for a moment. I could tell it was still hard for him to speak of her. "It was hard going on without her. There were so many things to remind me of her. The house, favorite restaurants, friends – all reminded me of her. So, I decided to move somewhere else and get a fresh start." He glanced my way. "That's why I'm here." He looked at Liz, "Any more questions?"

She looked embarrassed. And that's hard for Liz to do.

"Bob, I've been meaning to drop by and see your shop. Maybe I can get a tour of the place?" Pastor Steve tactfully changed the subject.

"Sure thing. This shop is only a baby compared to the factory in Madison, but come on by, and I'll show you around. I'll show you the relic of a chair your friend, Arthur, brought in. He must really believe in miracles if he thinks I can restore it. It's literally in pieces."

"Just so happens, some of us do believe in miracles," Pastor Steve said, as he stood to leave.

I smiled good-bye to him. But I thought I heard Pastor Steve mutter under his breath, "With God, all things are possible." (Mt:19:26 NIV)

Chapter 10

There was a church council meeting that night and it seemed to go on forever. How much time can one spend discussing new drapes for the pastor's office and the fellowship hall? You wouldn't think men would be at all particular, but when it comes to spending money, they suddenly become very interested.

Deacon Ed Hooper thought nice neutral brocade would be attractive. Obviously, his wife Louise, had been telling him what she thought would be nice. Elder Carl was against drapes at all, and favored plastic blinds that would last forever. Ben Adams, church treasurer, didn't care what we got, as long as the bill came in under $500. And Dwight Underwood submitted samples of a thermal lined, synthetic blend, from his nephew's drapery business. It was guaranteed against rot and mildew, and was sure to insulate against the cold, winter winds. Finally, at 10:00 p.m., the subject was delegated to a committee to make the final decision. Dwight Underwood volunteered to be committee chairman. That figured.

I stayed back to wash the coffee cups and put things away. I didn't want Martha to have to face cold coffee grounds and dirty cups, when she opened the office in the morning. I was the last one to leave, so I locked the door behind me.

Darn! I should have parked on the street instead of the parking lot. The flood lights were set to turn off at 10:00 pm, and there were not many lights on in the surrounding homes. Most people were in a nice, warm bed, where I should be.

Spring nights are still pretty chilly in Wisconsin. I was deep in thought about the flowers I had planted and worrying about frost. I was so busy looking for frost on the roof of my car, I didn't notice, right away, that my back tire was flat. So was the front; on both sides of the car. I looked around the deserted parking lot, suddenly feeling very frightened and vulnerable.

There was something white under the windshield wiper. My hands were shaking as I plucked the paper out. I could barely read the words in the dark, but the heavy black scrawl stood out against the white paper. "Mind your own business. Stop snooping or else." I stuffed it in my pocket, and fumbled with the car door remote. I could lock myself in the car and call for help on my cell phone. My trembling fingers were finding it hard to hit the right buttons on the remote.

Adrenalin took over as car headlights suddenly swept over me, and a car turned into the parking lot. I jumped into the car, and locked the door with hands shaking with fear. I looked around frantically for something to use as a weapon to defend myself as the car pulled alongside mine. A small can of hair spray was in the glove compartment. If I sprayed it right in someone's eyes...

"Emily, is that you?" Pastor Steve's voice sounded like an angelic choir to me. "Is something wrong?"

"Thank God, it's you!" My eyes were filling with tears, and I was laughing and crying at the same time. I rolled down the window. "Look at my tires! And there was a threatening note under the windshield wiper."

"Come. Get in my car," he ordered.

I obeyed at once, and he drove quickly out of the parking lot.

"I didn't know what to do," I said. "I'm so glad you came back. I was so scared."

"I forgot my glasses, and had to come back for them," Pastor Steve explained. "I'm taking you right down to the police station with that note. I don't like this at all, Emily."

"Me either," I agreed. "Will they believe me? What if they say I let the air out of my tires myself and wrote the note, too?"

"You couldn't have. I'll vouch for that. You drove your car to the meeting, and never left the room. You never had the opportunity to sabotage your own car."

Sheriff Doyle wasn't in his office at that late hour, and the officer on duty, a new rookie, was startled by the two unannounced visitors. He didn't seem to know what to do about the note. Pastor Steve suggested he file a report and be sure to show it to the Sheriff in the morning.

Pastor Steve started to drive me home. He said he'd have someone from the men's ministry take care of fixing the flat tires in the morning.

"Are you sure you want to stay alone tonight?" he asked. "Nancy would be glad to make up the guest room for you."

Murder at the Fancy Frills Tea Room

It was a very appealing invitation. I knew Crumpet would be fine till morning. My bravado vanished.

"You don't think she'd mind you bringing home someone this late at night?"

He turned the car around. "Not at all, you know Nancy; everything's a grand adventure to her."

He was right again. Nancy greeted me as if I'd come for a pajama party. "Oh, what fun. You can borrow my blue satin pajamas. Are you all right? Four flat tires! Oh, my! Let's have some hot chocolate and talk. Oh, and my pink robe will look stunning on you." She was like a human humming bird, darting from one subject to another and one room to another. She gathered night clothes, bedding, cups and saucers while turning down the bed and making hot chocolate all at the same time.

I began to calm down as we sat around the kitchen table, mugs of hot chocolate in hand. What good people, I thought. How blessed I am to have such good friends.

"I don't like this at all, Emily," Pastor Steve repeated.

"Tell me again, what was in the note?" asked Nancy.

"Mind your own business. Stop snooping around." I replied.

"I didn't mean to pry. It's alright if you don't want to tell me," Nancy turned away, obviously offended.

"No, no! I don't mean you! That's exactly what the note said." I repeated the words on the note again.

Nancy laughed. "I thought you were telling me to mind my own business."

"How many people knew you were doing any "snooping around?" Pastor asked.

"Well, let me retrace my footsteps. There's Liz, I told her about meeting Bob Jennings at the Harwood place."

"You met Bob out there! How exciting. I didn't know you and Bob-" Nancy began.

I stopped Nancy before she went any further in the wrong direction. "No, nothing like that. We met by accident. I went out there just to look around. And, uh, it just so happened that Bob was out there, too. He'd heard so much about the old mansion, he wanted to see the place for himself."

"Then what happened?" Nancy hunched forward, eager for the rest of the story.

"It rained, we got wet, and ran for home." I was clearly disappointing her.

"Go on. Who else?" Pastor Steve asked

"Well, let me see. I'd been to the gym. "

"Good for you. I love that place! What a good way to get rid of stress. Exercise is so good for you," Nancy beamed. How can anyone beam at 11:45 p.m.?

"Who was there?" Pastor asked, trying to keep me on track.

"Well, let me see, there was Candy, at the desk. And a new gal, Evelyn something or other, and oh, yes, Dorothy and Debbie."

Nancy chimed in, "Dorothy works at the Lake County News and Debbie's a teacher's aide at the school. They both know lots of people. They could have passed information on to anyone. Inadvertently, of course."

"And Martha knew I was asking you for help. I guess a lot of people knew," I admitted.

"Well, someone found out and didn't like it." Steve said. "But I found out something you will like."

"Hearing some good news tonight would be nice, "I said. Nancy smiled in agreement.

"I did some checking on my own yesterday. Called a few clergy friends in Madison. One of them knew the Jennings family, and put me in touch with their pastor. Seems Carol was a strong Christian lady. Attended church regularly, even taught Sunday School. Bob was never a strong church goer, but was there often enough for people to know him. Seems everything he told us today about himself is true alright. He ran a very large, very successful furniture manufacturing plant up there."

I breathed a sigh of relief and my heart did a little tap dance. So that's where his money came from. Good ol' hard work. He hadn't knocked off his wife for the insurance money, after all. Not that I ever believed that gossip, not me. Not for one moment.

"Who was that man who sat with Pat's daughter at the funeral?" asked Nancy. "He didn't look very – I mean he was kind of –"

"Different?" I finished the sentence for her. "Pat talked about Trina having a new boyfriend, and called him pond scum. Actually, I overheard Trina and him arguing with Pat. They wanted money from her. Maybe I should try to find out more about him." The words were barely out of my mouth when Pastor Steve corrected me.

"Oh, no, you don't, young lady. No more snooping around, remember? Let's leave it to the police. What we all need now is a good night's sleep."

But sleep didn't come easily that night. I tossed and turned, and thought about what might have happened if Pastor Steve hadn't come back for his glasses. He never did get them. I smiled at the memory of him trying to read the directions on the hot chocolate package. He'd finally given up, and just scooped spoonfuls into his cup. Who had threatened me? Was Crumpet lonely? Was Bob lonely? I hugged my pillow as I thought of Bob. I fell asleep praying.

Chapter 11

We were all awakened by the phone ringing persistently at seven a.m.

Liz's voice boomed over the phone. "Tomorrow! Tomorrow you're getting a security system. I know a guy that installs them and he owes me a favor."

I didn't bother asking how she knew I was at the Pastor's house. It seemed half the town owed her a favor and the other half kept her informed of every activity that happened within the county.

Funny how things seem safe and normal in the daylight. I was anxious to get home and resume my normal life. Nancy offered to drop me off on her way to an early morning yoga class. I assured Pastor Steve I'd be alright, and that it was best to act like nothing had happened. Anyway, I had to feed Crumpet.

The streets were quiet and peaceful as we drove. How could such evil violence take place in such a serene setting?

I opened the door and was greeted by a disturbed cat. She didn't know whether to be glad to see me, and the promise of food, or angry that she had been left alone all night. She decided to be happy to see me, and breakfast, and wrapped herself around my ankles, purring non-stop.

Murder at the Fancy Frills Tea Room

I headed for the shower, after giving her some long overdue attention. As I lathered myself in lavender scented soap, I thought about the day ahead and thanked God for another day. There were a lot of reservations at the tea room, and I needed to get a start on the scones and cookies. I'd have Marcie do the finger sandwiches and Liz could do the set ups when and if she came in. How I missed Pat! I even missed her grumbling and complaints. All these thoughts were racing around in my head like track stars in the quarter mile run.

It wasn't until I'd dressed and was downing my second cup of coffee that I remembered that I would see Bob today! Suddenly, the day seemed brighter. I settled down with bible and coffee for my daily time with the Lord. No matter how busy the day ahead looked, I never wanted to start it without spending time with the Lord first. I read, prayed, and placed the day, and all its cares, in the Lord's hands.

I walked the few blocks to the tea room, thinking how glad I'd be to get my car back. I let myself in the back door and noticed an old beat up truck in the parking space behind Arthur's shop. Maybe Arthur's car was in the shop and they'd given him an old truck as a loner. I'd have to kid him about it later. I smiled at the thought of sophisticated Arthur driving that old wreck.

I thought I heard loud male voices coming from next door, but as I entered the back room, they stopped. Some of Arthur's older customers were hard of hearing, making it necessary to raise one's voice, so I didn't give it another thought. Still, it was surprising that he'd have a customer this early. Oh, well, I had more important things on my mind.

I was busy chopping nuts for the white chocolate and pecan scones when Marcie arrived. "Who does that old beat up truck out there belong to?" she asked.

I glanced out the window at the truck and gasped in surprise.

"What's the matter?" Marcy came to my side. "Are you all right? You look like you just saw a ghost."

"It's Sammy!" I watched as he got into the truck, slammed the door and drove away. "That's Trina's boyfriend."

"You mean Pat's daughter?" Marcie asked.

"Yes."

"What would he be doing here?" she asked.

"I don't know." Was it his voice I heard coming from Arthur's shop? Why would Sammy be at Arthur's? Was he looking for me? My hands were shaking, and I didn't know why. I just knew something was very wrong. The sight of Sammy really unnerved me.

Marcie returned to making sandwiches and I started another batch of scones.

I placed the "Open" sign in the window about ten o'clock. Liz was the first one through the door. "Here I am!" she announced. "I cleared my schedule for most of the day. I only have one appointment at three, and I figured we'd be done by then. Right?" Every curl of her red hair was sprayed into perfect place and defied movement as she slipped an apron over her head, and around her ample frame.

"Three? Oh, yes, definitely. I have an appointment, too. You're a blessing to come in and help out like this. You, too, Marcie. I guess I better start looking for another part-time girl." I smiled at my two angels in disguise.

Marcie looked relieved. "I'm glad to hear that. I really can't work many more hours than I do now, with the family and all."

"I know, and I appreciate your helping out in this emergency." I gave her a grateful hug.

"Well, I'm having fun waiting on customers," Liz said "and I'll come in as much as I can, but I do have a real estate business to run, too. Sometimes it seems like it runs me." She sighed.

"I don't know how you do it all, Liz. You're the top sales person in the whole state," I said.

She grinned. "You better believe it. And when I sell that Harwood place – hey, want to go out there again with me? I've got the key!"

"That's what you said the last time, and look what happened. No thanks!"

Marcie interrupted us. "Liz, guess who we saw this morning?"

"I hate guessing games. Just tell me."

"Trina's boyfriend, Sammy," Marcie announced.

Liz choked on the cookie she was sampling. "Sammy? Here?" She looked at me for an explanation.

I nodded. "When I came to work this morning, there was an old truck sitting in back of Arthur's shop. It kind of looked familiar. I thought at first it was a loner, you know, while Arthur's car was in for repair or something."

Liz had stopped chewing. "And it was Sammy's?"

"Later on we saw Sammy get in and drive away," I told her.

"Did he come in here? Did he talk to you?"

Before I could answer, Marcie spoke up. "He was at Arthur's . We saw him leave."

"Marcie, we don't know that he was at Arthur's," I corrected her. We just saw him get in the truck and drive off."

"Well, he came from that direction," she defended herself. "Where else would he have been?"

"Doesn't sound like Sammy would have any reason to visit an antique store, from what I hear about him," Liz said.

We soon got busy with the noon hour rush, and I put Sammy and Arthur out of my mind, but not for long. Arthur came in about one o'clock for a sandwich to take to his shop. Marcie was busy waiting on tables, and Liz was fixing salads in the back room.

"Busy day today," he said, glancing around the crowded tea room. He smiled flirtatiously at an attractive, middle-aged woman.

"Yes, good thing I got an early start. Just like you did." I waited for his response.

"Oh, I slept in this morning," he said, examining the selection of scones. "Didn't get in to the shop until well after ten."

"Really? I thought maybe you had an early customer." I paused, then added, "Someone driving an old beat up truck."

Arthur frowned. "Must have been a customer for one of the other shops." He bent down and peered into the glass case holding the fresh scones and muffins. "Did you see who was driving it?" He avoided making eye contact with me.

A warning buzzer went off in the back of my mind. "I just got a glimpse as he drove away." I hope the Lord would forgive me for stretching the truth. It wasn't quite an out and out lie. "He looked like a creep."

Arthur laughed. "Then it wouldn't be one of my customers, dear. I only deal with elite society, so to speak. My customers are refined and sophisticated, like you, dear." He stroked my hand as he took the bag of scones he'd selected.

"How's business, Arthur?" Liz asked as she brought the salads up to the refrigerator case.

"Liz! You're working here?" Arthur looked shocked at the sight of Liz, the professional realtor, wearing an apron.

"Just helping out till Emily finds a replacement for Pat. It's actually fun for me. What's new with you?"

"The old is always new with me," Arthur smiled. "I'm getting in a new shipment of antiques from Germany in the next few days. Stop by and take a look."

"I'll do that. Say, I understand there are still a lot of good pieces out at the Bingham estate. You interested?" Liz placed menus on tables as she talked.

"Always interested in finding something rare and beautiful." He smiled at me and winked as he said it.

I could feel my face turning red. I wish he wouldn't flirt with me like that. I was sure he didn't mean anything by it, but still, it bothered me.

"I'll give you a call when they're ready to go to auction," she called after him as he left.

She looked at me. "Well?"

I wiped the counter. "I didn't tell him I saw Sammy."

"Why not?" she demanded.

"He said he didn't get in to open his shop till after ten. Said he didn't know anything about an old truck parked out there."

"Do you think he was telling the truth?" She looked as confused as I felt.

I had a strange feeling in the pit of my stomach and it wasn't from the scones I'd been sampling. I put down the tray of cranberry scones, fresh from the oven.

"I'm sure I heard voices coming from his place early this morning, when I first came in. And it really did look like Sammy came from Arthur's shop. I mean, we didn't see him come out of Arthur's back door exactly, but..."

"You know what? I think this whole thing has unnerved you. And I don't blame you," Liz interrupted. "You're worried about all that has happened. Two murders are enough to upset anyone, especially when one of them is your business partner. Then, hearing voices from next door, and seeing Sammy – maybe it wasn't even him. It might have been someone who looked like him. Arthur would have no reason to lie about Sammy. What would Arthur have to do with a low life like Sammy, anyway? Just forget the whole thing."

Murder at the Fancy Frills Tea Room

The phone interrupted us and I went to answer it. It's true, I had a lot on my mind and I was worried about many things. In addition to all that was going on, I needed to prepare my talk on the health benefits of tea for the women's club. They had booked me months ago. I couldn't let them down. I was probably just imagining things about Sammy, blowing them way out of perspective. Or was I?

Chapter 12

I knew exactly where Bob's shop was located. I knew practically every street in our little town. I was sure I wouldn't have any trouble finding the address, and I was right. A huge sign "JENNINGS CUSTOM FURNITURE" was displayed over the front of a large one story brick commercial building. I parked in front of the door, in one of the lanes marked "Visitors."

The door opened into a pleasant reception room. Warm wood paneling covered the walls. A leather sofa and loveseat offered seating, and there was a coffee table with a pretty potted plant adorning it. A congratulations card peeked out of the foliage. The fragrance of wood and sawdust filled the room. I looked around for a bell or buzzer to announce my arrival. There was none. I wasn't sure if I should just wait to see if anyone came out of the adjoining factory or what to do. After a few minutes of indecision, I opened the factory door and called Bob's name.

The whirring of a machine stopped at the sound of my voice. "Hello? Bob called back.

"Hi, It's me – Emily," I called into the depths of the huge room.

Murder at the Fancy Frills Tea Room

He came walking out from behind a row of machines, wearing a canvas apron over his clothes. There was sawdust in his hair and a big grin on his face. "Come on in. I'm glad you came. Wasn't sure if you really would." He smiled down at me.

I was trying to think of something clever to say, but my tongue seemed to be glued to the roof of my mouth. I just stood there like an idiot gazing into those beautiful deep brown eyes of his.

"Come on, I'll show you around." He took my arm and guided me, as he talked. "We're not up to speed yet, so I haven't hired anyone. With a little luck, I'll soon be putting some men to work, though."

He gave me a tour of the whole work area, explaining things like routers, orbit sanders and tongue and groove assembly. He talked about different types of woods and how each was best used. There was pride and passion in his voice and I could tell that he loved his work. I'm sure if I had been able to concentrate, it would have been very educational. But every time he touched my shoulder to guide me towards another machine, or took my hand to lead me down a row, my mind turned to Jello.

Finally, he said, "So, what do you think of it all?"

"Wonderful!" I swallowed hard. What a dumb thing to say. "I mean – you've done so much in such a short time. All this equipment."

He frowned. "It's nothing compared to what my factory in Madison was. But in time, I'll build it up again."

I was going to ask him what he meant, when he abruptly changed the subject. "Look at these pieces your friend, Arthur, brought in." He held a box of junk for me to look at.

"What is it?" I eyed the assortment of wood pieces.

"When – or maybe I should say if – I can put it together, it will be a Queen Anne chair from the 14th century. See, these three pieces form the seat, and this is a leg, and ...I'm not sure what this one is yet." He held up what looked to me like a drumstick.

I laughed. "Well, if anyone can do it, you can. I have faith in you."

"Do you, Emily?" He looked very serious for a moment, and then laughed. "Well, I'll do the best I can." He put the box down. "Speaking of faith, another friend of yours came by today, too."

"Oh?" I looked up at him.

"Pastor Steve stopped in this morning. We had a long talk. Nice guy."

"The best," I agreed. "By the way, the church is having a pot luck after church, this Sunday. Lots of good food. Would you like to come?"

"Sunday?" He hesitated. I held my breath. "Well, I guess I could do that. Not doing anything else. Should I bring something?"

"Oh, good!" I hope I didn't sound too excited. "You won't have to bring a thing. I'll fix enough for both of us." This was going better than I could believe. But it didn't last long.

"Emily, I just noticed the time. I've got an appointment I've got to keep." He took me by the arm and steered me toward the front door. I was getting the bum's rush!

"Oh, well – sorry to have taken so much of your time," I stammered. What had I done, I wondered, to turn him off?

"Please don't be offended. It's just something I have to do and I can't be late."

"I understand," I said coolly, even though I didn't.

"I don't think you do." He took my hand. "How about having dinner with me tomorrow night to make up for having to cut this visit short?"

My icy tone vanished. "I'd love to."

"Pick you up about 6:30," he said as he opened the door for me.

I didn't even notice how quickly he closed it. I just floated out to my car. I was going to have dinner with Bob Jennings. And he had held my hand!

As I drove away I glanced in my rear view mirror. I saw Bob run to his car and speed away in the direction of the freeway. I couldn't help but wonder, what was his important appointment?

*****

Crumpet was glad to see me. I'd been spending so much more time at the shop than usual; she probably felt she'd been abandoned. I picked her up and did a little dance around the room. "I'm having dinner with Bob Jennings" I sang to the tune of "I'm Getting Married in the Morning" from "My Fair Lady." For a moment, I even felt like Audrey Hepburn, till I caught a glimpse of my foolish self in the mirror, twirling around the room.

Audrey Hepburn could look gorgeous dressed in rags, but not me! What would I wear tomorrow night? I hadn't been on an evening dinner date for so long, I didn't know if I even had anything suitable. I opened the closet doors, still holding Crumpet in my arms.

A row of jeans and pants hung before me. Sweatshirts, T shirts and a denim jacket hung above them. On the other side of the closet were my "Go to Meetin'" clothes, a navy suit and a few dresses. Nothing glamorous, nothing that would make me look beautiful. I selected a print dress and held it up to me. I looked in the mirror and my eyes shifted from the dress to my hair. What would I do with my hair? I had meant to get it cut last week, but since Pat's death, nothing had gone as planned.

"Oh, Lord, what have I gotten myself into?" I flopped down on my bed. My joy had turned to despair. Crumpet curled up against me. I picked up my bible. Did God have any advice on what to wear to attract a man? The pages fell open to Phillippians, chapter 4. There my eyes rested upon verse 19, and I chuckled as I read: "*I tell you, do not worry about your life, what you will eat or drink, or about your body, what you will wear. Is not life more important than food, and the body more important than clothes? Look at the birds of the air, they do not sow or reap or store away in barns, and yet your heavenly Father feeds them. Are you not much more valuable than they*?" God surely has a sense of humor.

I looked again at my closet. God had been faithful in clothing me every day. Any one of the things I would wear to church would be just fine to wear to dinner.

Thinking about dinner made me realize I was hungry. Probably Crumpet was, too. I fed Crumpet first, and looked over the selection of fine dining gourmet meals that awaited me in the freezer. I selected a frozen entrée and hoped it tasted as good as the picture looked.

After my disappointing dinner I tried to settle down with a magazine, but my mind kept playing hopscotch. Who killed Pat? Was there a connection to the body found at the Harwood mansion? Why was Sammy's truck at Arthur's place, and why did Arthur lie? What should I wear to dinner tomorrow night?

I knew sleep would not come easily to my over worked mind, so I fixed a cup of Sleepytime tea and went to bed. The tea worked.

✳✳✳✳✳

The morning passed in a flurry of scones, tea sandwiches, red hats and feathers. Yes, feathers. One of the red hat ladies topped off her purple dress with a long, red feather boa. She took great joy in dramatically flipping it over her shoulder. When she wasn't flipping, she was twirling one end of it ala Gypsy Rose Lee. She left a trail of red feathers wherever she twirled, flipped or tripped. The light little feathers floated through the air onto surrounding tables, into customer's salads, and even made it as far back as the work room, where they landed on a fresh batch of scones, hot from the oven.

Things finally slowed down about 1:30 and that's when Liz arrived. "Yoo-hoo, Emily, are you back there?" she called to the back room, where I was busy cleaning up. "I want you to meet someone."

I wiped my hands on my apron, and prepared myself to meet what I knew must be the next in a long line of men that Liz persisted in digging up for me. So far, she had unearthed a gambler, a scam artist, an obese plumber, a cross dresser and a retired general who was still giving orders. Did I mention Liz was not always a good judge of character? I kept telling her I could only be interested in a Christian man, but Liz always countered that if they weren't Christian, I could convert them.

"There you are, darling," she said as I came through the archway. She took me by the arm and hurried me over to a table where a nice looking, older man sat. "I want you to meet Dr. Frank Hanson. Frank, this is my little sister, Emily." She beamed at us. I half expected her to pull out Cupid's bow and arrow from her bag, she was so obvious.

I gave her one of my "what are you getting me into" looks and smiled weakly at Frank. He pulled out a chair for me; a gentleman of the old school.

"I've heard so much about you," he smiled. Nice teeth. His own?

"Frank's been looking at properties all morning. He's considering the Morgan estate or one of the new homes in the Silverwoods area." In other words, he's a millionaire. I got the message. So did Frank.

"Well, if you've been traipsing in and out of houses all morning, you must be famished. Can I offer you some lunch? We still have some sandwiches, but I'm afraid the soup is all gone."

"How kind of you. If it's not too much trouble, a cup of coffee would be fine," Frank said. Then he remembered he was in a tea shop. "Oh, I forgot. You probably don't have coffee – this is a tea room!"

Murder at the Fancy Frills Tea Room

"If you promise not to tell anyone, we do have a pot of coffee in the back room. I'll be glad to get you a cup, but you'll have to take an oath of secrecy," I responded.

"Scout's honor," he said as he raised three fingers on his right hand.

I pulled my tummy in as I walked to the coffee pot. May as well try to make a nice impression. I watched him as I poured coffee into a pretty china mug. He had silver white hair, a well-trimmed mustache, and a very nice smile. He looked to be about six feet tall, though it was hard to tell when he was sitting down. At least he wasn't obese, like the plumber. He must be well educated, if he were a Doctor and millionaire. I decided to go all out and put a few sandwiches and cookies on a plate to accompany the coffee. Liz could drink peach tea.

They were talking about Pat as I put the food and drinks before them. "Any news?" Liz asked.

"No, haven't heard a word." I set the food before them.

Frank looked concerned. "It must be very difficult for you."

I nodded. "What is your specialty, Dr.?" I wanted to change the subject to something more pleasant.

"Orthopedics. I'm retired now, but still do some consulting and lecturing."

"Isn't that interesting!" Liz crowed. "No wonder you have such nice teeth."

Frank looked puzzled.

"That's orthodontics," I said, giving her a kick under the table. "Orthopedics is working with bones, right, Dr.?"

"Call me Frank, please. Yes, I specialize in injuries and conditions involving bones, but also connective tissue, tendons and ligaments."

"Oh, well, you have nice bones, too." Liz laughed.

Frank smiled, leaned toward me and said, "May I?" I held my breath as he reached out to me – and plucked a red feather from my hair. "I've been wondering what this was ever since I first saw you."

And I thought he was studying me because he was genuinely interested. My ego deflated like a popped balloon. I explained the source of the red feather, and we all laughed as I imitated the red hat lady's flip and twirl.

I glanced at the clock and was surprised to see how fast the time had gone. I was enjoying the visit with Frank and Liz, but I had a lot of cleaning up to do before I could go home and get ready for my big dinner date with Bob.

Liz came to the rescue when she remembered another appointment she had.

"Well, since I don't have my own car here, I guess I'll have to leave with Liz". He sounded disappointed. Was he hinting that I should take him home?

"Yes, and I have a lot of work to do before I can leave." I stood up. "It was nice meeting you."

He extended his hand, and held my hand firmly as we shook hands. He looked directly into my eyes and said, "I hope to see you again, Emily."

"That would be nice," I answered.

That might be very nice, I thought, as I watched him open the car door for Liz and help her in. Very nice, indeed.

Murder at the Fancy Frills Tea Room

I flipped the sign that read "Sorry you can't come for tea, We are closed as you can see." And with a sigh of relief locked the door. I'd made it through another day without Pat. I started cleaning up, putting things away and planning for the next day.

I was surprised when I heard a knock on the door. "Can't you see we're closed?" I said to myself. But, when I turned to the door, I saw it was Marcie. She smiled and motioned to me to let her in.

"I had a feeling you'd still be here," she said as I opened the door.

"My home away from home," I said wearily.

"It's really tough without Pat, isn't it?" she sympathized.

"I guess I never appreciated all that she did. You know how it is, things get done and you don't stop to think about all that went into it. I even miss her grumbling."

Marcie laughed. "I know. She could complain about anything. But, you know, underneath it all, she had a heart of gold."

"Like feeding every stray animal that came her way. Remember that little dog that got hit by a car out in front of the tearoom? She was the one that took it to the vet, and paid the bill for it, too," I recalled.

"Did you know she paid for Debbie's braces when I couldn't afford them?" Marcie asked. "The dentist said if we didn't get Debbie into braces within the next year it would take twice as long to correct, and twice as expensive. I came to work all upset about it, because we didn't have the money for it. When Pat asked me what was bothering me, I told her what was going on. The next thing I knew, I got a call from the dentist saying to bring Debbie in, the braces were all paid for."

"Really?" I was shocked. "I never knew that! How generous of her."

"She didn't want anyone to know." Her voice broke. She blinked away a few tears that were forming in her eyes. Then, she held out a package to me. "I almost forgot the reason I came by. This sweater was given to me and its way too small for me. I've got to lose some weight! But I thought it might be just the right size for you."

I opened the bag and pulled out a beautiful, pale blue sweater. It was a nice, light weight, year round, elegant style. I held it up to me, and it looked like it would fit.

"It's definitely your color," Marcie exclaimed. "It brings out the color of your eyes, and skin tone."

"I love it," I said, stroking the soft knit. It would be perfect to wear tonight with the skirt from my navy blue suit. "How much do I owe you for it?"

"Not a thing. Like I said, it was given to me and I couldn't wear it."

"I couldn't just take it. I have to give you something in return," I argued.

"Well, if you insist, how about a movie some night? It would be a real treat to get out of the house and away from the kids."

"You got it!" I gave Marcie a hug.

"Let me give you a hand cleaning up," she said. "I don't have to be home for the kids for another hour or so."

Murder at the Fancy Frills Tea Room

What a blessing from God she was. Together, we sailed through the closing routine and I was soon on my way home to prepare for the first real date I'd had in months.

I gathered together the things I had to take home, and headed for the door. In my haste, I dropped my keys and as I bent to retrieve them, I bumped my crazy bone on a wrought iron chair. True to its name, it hurt like crazy.

Is there's really a bone with that name? I'll have to ask Frank. That's when it hit me. Suddenly, there were two men in my life! I had to admit there was something about Frank that I found very attractive, too. Was I being influenced by his money?

I'd been thinking I'd never find a nice man, and suddenly God had put two of them in my life.

"Hmmm, what's up, God?" I said aloud.

He didn't answer.

Chapter 13

The waiter led us to a table on the far side of the popular restaurant. I stretched to my full height as I walked in front of Bob, following the waiter. I wanted to look as thin and elegant as possible. He'd already complemented me on my appearance. Things were going well, so far. Now, if I could only keep from dumping my dinner in my lap!

"Something to drink?" the waiter asked. "Cocktails, a bottle of wine, perhaps?"

"Raspberry ice tea for me," I answered, wondering what Bob would order.

"I'd like that, too," Bob said. I breathed a sigh of relief. The last date I'd had was offended when I didn't want to join him in drinking cocktails.

We looked at each other across the table. For the life of me, I couldn't think of anything to say. He seemed to be having the same problem. Should I tell him all the reasons he should drink at least four cups of tea a day? Would he like to know that ice tea has all the benefits of hot tea? I smiled. He smiled back.

I glanced around the room. There weren't many nice eating places in Riverbend, mostly just fast food places. The table next to ours was occupied by a family with three children. Not a very romantic setting, but it sure beat another night of Lean Cuisine.

I felt a hand on my shoulder, and turned to look into Arthur's smiling face. "Well, look who's here," he said, leering at us.

"Hello, Arthur," Bob responded.

"Hi, Arthur. Where's Sue?" I hoped he wasn't going to pull out a chair and sit down with us.

"Ladies room. We were just leaving, but I saw you two and had to say hello. Bob, have you had time to look at that chair, yet?" His hand was still on my shoulder. "I found the most magnificent old English chair, Emily, from the 17th century. Wait till you see it."

"Actually, she has seen it." Bob smiled at me.

"You mean those pieces of wood? I thought you were joking. That's really supposed to be a chair?" I wished he would remove his hand from my shoulder.

"Those 'pieces of wood' are solid Black Forest walnut, my dear." His fingers moved down my back in a soft caress.

"I have some other things I want to bring over, too," he said to Bob. "An armoire and a desk. I'm not sure they'll fit in my van, I may have to borrow a truck."

"There you are!" Sue said as she approached us. Arthur's hand dropped to his side. "Have you ordered yet? We had the prime rib, it was delicious."

"I was considering that," I smiled back.

"Any more news? Pat's death is the talk of the town. That and that awful other murder." Seemed Sue wanted to visit, too. I hoped they would move on.

"Come on, we have to go, Arthur interrupted. "Nice seeing you two."

"Bye," Sue waved as he headed her towards the door. We watched them leave.

The waiter came to take our order and we both chose the prime rib.

"Arthur's van must not be running," Bob said as he drank his ice tea.

"Arthur doesn't have a truck. I think he was trying to find out if you had one he could borrow."

"Oh? I saw an old truck parked in back of his place late one night, and I just assumed it was his." He unfolded his napkin.

Bells clanged in my head. "What kind of old truck? When?"

"Just a few nights ago. I didn't pay much attention to it. It just seemed out of place, you know. Didn't fit in with Arthur's persona."

"You said it was late at night?" I asked.

"Yes." He looked uncomfortable. "I, uh, was coming home from a, uh, meeting, and just happened to notice it."

"Well, hello! How nice to run into you!" a woman's voice said.

I looked up to see Jean Wilcox beaming at me. "I've been wanting to call you. I want to invite you to a little gathering I'm hosting next week, on Wednesday evening. You can bring your friend…" She looked inquiringly at Bob.

"Jean, this is Bob Jensen." I had no choice but to introduce him.

Before I could finish the introduction, she quickly shook his hand and gushed "Oh, it's so nice to meet you! I do hope you'll come to my little party, too. It will be so much fun, entertaining and informative. You be sure to bring him, Emily. You've turned me down the last few invitations. Now don't disappoint me. It's at seven, sharp."

Bob looked at me in confusion.

"I must run. Bye! Don't forget. Seven sharp!" She disappeared as quickly as she had appeared.

"That was very friendly of her, inviting a perfect stranger to her party," Bob said as he watched her leave.

I couldn't help laughing. "You've just met the Queen of network marketing. Her so called parties are just a ruse to get people to come to her house so she can give them an hour long presentation on her latest multi-level marketing program. So far, she's gone through water filters, phone cards and diet food. I'm not sure what the latest 'opportunity of a life time' is. That's why I keep turning down her invitations."

"I see. I think I just remembered I'll be busy next Wednesday night," he said rolling his eyes.

"Wise decision," I agreed. "I'm sure I'll be busy, too."

"How long have you lived in Riverbend, Emily?" he asked.

I wanted to go back to the conversation we were having, before Jean interrupted us. I was curious as to what kind of meeting he'd attended that ended late at night, but it would have been awkward to do so, so I answered his question instead.

"Liz talked me into coming here, after the company I was working for, folded. I felt I needed to make a change, and thought it would be nice to be close to the only family I had. Liz and I have always been close, even though we're so different. I'm glad I made the move. I love it here."

"Did I hear my name mentioned?" a familiar voice said.

I almost choked on my prime rib.

It was Liz and Roger. "How nice to see you two," she grinned. Her charm bracelets rattled as she adjusted the flaming pink scarf around her neck. "I told Roger I thought I saw you come in. We were sitting on the other side, and Roger had to finish his dessert before we could come over and say hello." She waved at an acquaintance across the room, rattling her bracelets again. Then she ran her tongue over her teeth and smiled at me.

Roger removed the toothpick from his mouth. "Don't believe we've met," he said, extending his hand to Bob. "I'm Roger Comstead, Liz's husband."

Bob stood, and shook hands with Roger. "Bob Jennings."

Before he could say anything else, Liz took over. "This is the one I told you about, Rog. He's the furniture manufacturer. Bought the building over on Water St." Then she brought her finger to her mouth and rubbed a tooth. I remembered she'd missed a dental appointment, and supposed she had a tooth that was now bothering her.

More pleasantries were exchanged and they finally left. Liz gave me a glance of matchmaker victory over her shoulder as she paraded out of the restaurant, still rubbing her tooth.

Murder at the Fancy Frills Tea Room

I wasn't going to order dessert, but Bob insisted. I'd managed to eat my whole dinner without dropping anything on my new sweater, and I didn't want to take any more chances.

Bob ordered pie, and I couldn't resist the tempting picture in the menu and ordered a slice of coconut cream pie. Of course, I didn't really want it. I just ordered pie to please Bob. Yeah, sure.

Your Pastor came by to visit me," Bob said between forkfuls.

"Pastor Steve? He's a great friend." I contemplated the pie. Should I eat the crust, too?

"We had a long talk." He paused. "About God."

My fork stopped in midair. "Oh?" I finally managed to say. I hoped he was going to tell me he had asked Jesus into his life.

"Guess I'm still kind of angry with God." He looked down at his half empty plate.

"Do you want to talk about it?"

"I'll tell you what I told him. I was married to a wonderful woman. She was kind, went to church, like you. We had a great life together. And then, all of a sudden, she was gone. Killed instantly, by a drunk driver running a traffic light. Hit her car broadside." His voice cracked. "Why would a loving God let something like that happen? Where was God when she needed him?"

I gulped. "What did Pastor Steve say?"

"Oh, he gave me some song and dance about God being right there with her, loving her into his kingdom." He looked away.

I nodded my head. "I believe God was there, Bob. We never know why these things happen. We just know that we live in an imperfect world, and accidents do happen. Jesus never promised us we wouldn't go through tragedies or difficult times, but he did promise us he would never leave us or forsake us."

"Yeah, that's about what Steve said. "Then he, uh, well, to tell you the truth, he kind of made me mad." He pushed his plate away.

"What happened?" I couldn't imagine Pastor Steve provoking Bob.

Bob leaned forward, an intense look of pain on his face. "That drunk driver, the guy that killed my wife and ruined my life, got off with only five years in jail. Is that justice? But your Pastor says I should forgive the guy. Can you imagine? I should forgive him..." He threw his napkin down in disgust.

What could I say? I didn't want him to be mad at me too, but I knew in my heart Pastor Steve was right. How could I explain to Bob that hating someone is like taking poison and expecting someone else to die.

"Emily?" I turned my head to see who had called my name.

"I thought it was you," Frank Hanson smiled at me.

"Oh, hello!" I was surprised to see him.

Bob stood up as I introduced the two men to each other.

Murder at the Fancy Frills Tea Room

"Bob, this is Dr. Frank Hanson, a new resident of Riverbend. This is Bob, uh – "my mind went completely blank. I couldn't think of Bob's last name! I felt like an idiot.

"Bob Jennings," Bob came to my rescue. "Pleased to meet you."

The two men stood staring at each other. Was Frank waiting for an invitation to join us? He wasn't going to get it from me.

"I'd invite you to join us, but we were just finishing," Bob finally said, as he sat down.

Frank answered politely, "I was on my way out, just wanted to say hello to Emily. Nice meeting you, he nodded to Bob. "Nice seeing you again," he said to me with a smile.

As he left, I said, "Is there a sign that says "Stop here as you exit? " I tried to make a joke of all the interruptions.

"I'm beginning to think so. Not a very quiet evening, is it?" The child in the high chair next to our table dropped a toy on the floor and started fussing. It seemed like a good time to leave.

Chapter 14

After changing into my comfy pj's, I curled up with Crumpet on my lap and sipped a cup of hot tea, while I tried to put sense and order into all that had happened lately. It was a cool, breezy spring night, and the gusts of wind were playing tricks on my imagination. Every creak and rattle in my little house was intensified. I reassured myself that it was just a branch on the maple tree outside the kitchen window that was making that tapping noise. I was glad that I had agreed to the security system that had been installed. Liz had insisted on it, and as usual, she was right; I felt less vulnerable.

Pat's murder just didn't make sense to me. I still had a hard time calling it murder, but that's what it was. I had to face the fact that someone had shot her, and left her body in the trunk of her car. I held Crumpet against me. And someone had stabbed her ex-husband to death at the old Harwood mansion. What was the connection between the two deaths?

Crumpet was unhappy when the phone rang and I had to disturb her to answer it.

"So, what's going on between you and Bob? " Like the inquiring tabloids, Liz wanted to know.

"Hello to you, too. Did you enjoy your dinner?"

"Don't try to change the subject. You two looked very cozy," Liz teased.

"Well, it was nice," I admitted. "Before the steady stream of table hoppers."

"Are you going out again? Did he make another date with you?"

"If he asks me. When I got home I discovered poppy seed between my teeth. I'm sure that made a good impression," I lamented. "Why didn't you tell me?"

"How could I work that into the conversation? I tried to send a few subtle hints, but you had too many stars in your eyes to see them. Why do you think I kept pointing to my teeth? I've been meaning to tell you it's a good idea not to eat spinach or poppy seed rolls on a date."

"Thanks a lot."

"Hey, I've got a prospect for the Harwood place!" Her voice rose in excitement. "Looks pretty good, too."

"Hope it's somebody with money," I said.

"Want to go out there with me, when I show it? The appointment is tomorrow, but not till four p.m. You'll be out of the tea room by then."

I thought about it. The mansion had been a real beauty in it's heyday, and I loved the glory of the old place. If I could forget the memory of the dead body in the basement, it might be fun to see its faded splendor again. "Maybe." I hesitated. "Yeah, I'll try to make it."

"Tell me what you think of Frank," she changed subjects faster than a team at Nascar changed tires. "Isn't he handsome?"

"In an elderly way, I suppose. He's too old for me, don't you think?" A picture of his white hair came into my mind.

"Don't hold his age against him. He's young at heart, and has all that money, "she argued.

"Yes, but – "

"And he asked a lot of questions about you. I think he's interested in you." Liz wasn't about to give up.

"Really?" I was glad she couldn't see me beginning to blush.

After we hung up, I got ready for bed. I was glad to have Crumpet's company, as she curled up against me. I fell asleep thinking about the scripture, "The Lord is my strength and my shield; my heart trusts in him, and He helps me." (Ps 28:7 NIV)

✳✳✳✳✳

The next day I headed for the shop, determined to work through the list of things I had to do. Set interviews for a full time cook/baker/kitchen magician. Check all supplies and place food orders. The big cooler needed cleaning, and I noticed the front windows needed to be washed and the flower boxes tended to. I would have to consider menu changes as well. Some of Pat's special dishes were impossible to duplicate. How I missed my dependable partner.

I unlocked the front door and stepped inside. I left the Closed sign up, but decided to leave the door unlocked for the UPS man. I took a moment to just stand there and immediately a flood of memories washed over me. Pat grumbling about the tea accessories and gift items. Pat playing the music on the radio in the back room. Pat feeding every stray animal within a ten mile radius. Pat filling the display case with scones and cookies.

"All right. Get busy," I told myself. And I did. I cleaned and I cried. I ordered supplies and I cried a little more. It was the first time I really cried for Pat. The shock of her death and the mystery surrounding it suddenly overwhelmed me. Now, here in our beloved tea room, the tears were coming. I let them come. It felt good in a funny sort of way. By the time I finished cleaning the cooler, I had let it all out. I would miss her, yes, but I would go on. Pat would want me to do so. She wouldn't want me to be carrying on like a cry-baby. I squared my shoulders and checked off "clean cooler" on my list.

"Shouldn't leave your door unlocked like that," a voice said.

I looked up – at Sammy!

"What are you doing here?" I demanded. "What do you want?"

"Just thought we should have a little talk," he answered.

"About what? Is Trina with you?" I asked.

"Nope. It's just you and me." I didn't like his grin.

"What do you want?" I tried to keep my voice strong and confident and not betray my shaking knees.

"I just wanted to make sure you didn't tell the police about that little argument you heard us having with Pat, when you were spying on us the other day."

"I wasn't spying."

"Did you tell the police?" He took a step closer.

"I don't remember what I told them. They asked questions, I answered them." That was the truth. I had been so shocked to learn of Pat's death, I didn't remember what was actually said.

"Well, maybe you better remember. Remember that it was just a little misunderstanding. We were just a little upset, you know how it is. Sometimes you say things you don't really mean when you're upset." He picked up a knife from the work bench and stroked its blade. "You know how that is, don't you?"

Well, I sure knew I was being threatened. What should I do? Where was that burly UPS man when you needed him? What would Pat do if she were here? I squared my shoulders and looked for a way to defend myself. A scripture flashed through my mind. "No weapon formed against you will prevail." (Is 54:17 NIV). Courage welled up inside me, and I was surprised to hear my voice demanding "Are you trying to threaten me? You take one step towards me and I'll scream so loud every cop in the county will hear me. The wrath of God be upon you!" Was that voice really coming from me? And I actually took a step towards him.

Sammy turned as white as the flour on the work bench. He seemed to be looking at something or someone behind me. An angel, perhaps?

He dropped the knife to the floor. "No, no. I'm not threatening you. Not at all. I, uh, I just wanted you to know I didn't mean nothin' about what I said that day." He started to back away, towards the door.

"Get out of here! And don't come back!" I yelled at him.

He ran out the door and disappeared quickly down the street. I watched him turn the corner. I didn't see his truck anywhere.

"Thank you, Lord," I said and collapsed in a chair.

I jumped to my feet as the door opened again. Was he back?

"Are you alright, Emily? I just saw a strange man run out of here." It was Arthur. "You're shaking," he continued. "What was he doing here? Did he hurt you?"

"No, Arthur, I'm alright. I think he just wanted to scare me."

"Looks like he did." Arthur looked worried. "Who was that man, anyway? What did he want?"

"It was Trina's boyfriend. I overheard an argument between him, Pat and Trina shortly before Pat was killed. I took a deep breath and tried to compose myself. "The creep."

"Yes. Sammy looks like an unsavory person." Arthur agreed.

"I don't know what Trina sees in him," I pondered.

"What was the argument about?" Arthur asked.

"Money. They wanted money from Pat."

"Pat had money?" Arthur sounded surprised.

"They seemed to think so. I wonder if that's why she was killed." I leaned against a table for support.

"Now, Trina gets her money," Arthur mused. He smiled. "Well, no doubt the police will sort it all out." He looked at me tenderly. "You sure you're all right? Can I get you anything?" He put his arm around me and tried to pull me to him.

"No, I'm fine," I said, turning away. Being threatened and having a pass made at me, all in the same fifteen minutes, was more than I could take.

"I have a lot of work to do." I reached for the broom. "Is that your phone I hear ringing?"

"You can hear things from my shop over here?" He looked surprised.

"These walls are pretty thin. You'd be surprised what I hear," I answered, trying to lighten the mood.

"Well, if you're sure you're alright then," he said, heading for the door.

I locked it after he left. I didn't want any more unexpected visitors. The UPS man would just have to pound on the door. Serve him right for not showing up when he was needed!

Chapter 15

I got up early the next morning and headed for the fitness center. I better pay better attention to my fitness or it would soon be non-existent.

The music hit me in the face when I opened the door. Females of assorted sizes and shapes were moving to its rhythm. I found a spot and joined in. I liked to think of it as a magic time, where miracles happened. Fat disappeared, and muscle appeared out of thin space. I looked around, and was glad to see Judy.

"How are you doing?" she called over the music. "Everything going OK?" She knew I'd been working overtime, keeping things going at the tearoom.

I smiled. "I'm interviewing today for some extra help."

"Good prospects?" she moved to the next machine.

"I hope so," I answered.

"I hear you've got a new boyfriend." She never missed a beat as she exercised and talked at the same time.

"Don't believe everything you hear, Judy," I said.

"Well, half the town is buzzing about it," she said in a hurt tone. "Least you could have done is tell me about it. I'm supposed to be your best friend, or so I thought."

"Course you are," I reassured her. "I've just been so busy trying to keep things going, without Pat, I haven't had time to call you or anyone. To bring you up to date, I just had dinner with Bob Jennings. That's all. There's no big romance. But, kind of wish there were," I added.

Martha and Meg, the dynamic duo, were on the other side of the circle. I could overhear Meg telling her Mother all about the retired rich Dr. that was buying a home on Meadowlark Lane.

"Have you met him?" Judy nodded her head in their direction. "The Doctor they're talking about?"

"Yes. Liz introduced us. She was showing him properties. Very rich. Very nice. Very old." I tried to catch my breath.

"She brought him into the library, too. He seemed very nice, and not too old. Good looking, I thought. I didn't realize he was rich, though. I should have been nicer." She moved from an ab machine to one that worked the inner thighs.

"You're always nice," I reassured her.

"I hear you're getting a new neighbor, next door to your tea shop," Martha said to me, as she headed for the water cooler.

"Who, me?" She must have me mixed up with someone else. Arthur's Antique shop and Betty's Boutique were my neighbors, and neither of them were moving.

"That antique store next to your tearoom is for sale," Martha said knowingly.

"Arthur and Sue's place?" I was dumbfounded. "You must be mistaken. They've never said a word to me about wanting to sell. And Liz would certainly tell me if they contacted her."

"She's not the only realtor around," Martha said defensively. "It just so happens that my niece is a realtor, too, over in Westport, and that's who they listed with."

"But, why would they – why wouldn't they tell me?" I looked at Judy for support. I couldn't believe Arthur was selling his business.

"News to me," she said.

My niece just got the listing last night," Martha added triumphantly.

Liz would be devastated. Imagine Arthur going to another realtor! And an out of town realtor, at that. I could hardly wait to tell her. It wasn't often I knew something before she did.

✳✳✳✳✳

The phone was ringing as I unlocked the door to the tea room.

"Did you know Arthur wanted to sell his shop?" Liz demanded.

"I just heard about it," I answered. "I can't believe it." I stashed my purse under the counter, and headed for the back room.

"The traitor!" Liz was mad. "How dare he list with an out of town realtor. That's like a slap in the face. No one sells more commercial properties than I do in the whole county!"

"Maybe he didn't want you to know," I offered meekly. I didn't understand why he didn't list with Liz, either. She was a genius at selling her listings.

"Oh, by the way, any new developments about the murders?" Liz jumped from one subject to another faster than a twelve year old jumping rope.

I told her about Sammy's surprise visit, and how Arthur had come rushing over.

"Wow! Good for you, girl! I can't believe you stood up to Sammy like that." She hesitated. It sounded like she was eating something. "Are you sure you told me word for word what happened, and what you told Arthur?"

"It's pretty fresh in my memory. Why?"

"Well, think back. Did you mention Sammy by name, or just refer to him as Trina's boyfriend?"

The whole incident played out in my memory again. "I think I see what you're getting at. If I never mentioned Sammy by name, how did Arthur know who it was?. He definitely said "Sammy looks like an unsavory person. Only Arthur would describe someone as unsavory."

"He should have said 'that creep looks like an unsavory person' or something like that." More chewing sounds from Liz. "Well, maybe he met him at Pat's funeral service."

"Hmmm, maybe. But Sammy's not the kind of person Arthur would care to be introduced to. You know how he is."

"But if he knows Sammy, it would explain why Sammy's truck was outside his shop." Now it sounded like she was drinking something.

"I gotta get busy and find out about his selling the business," she said, changing subjects again. "See you this afternoon?"

I remembered then about the Harwood place. "I'll try to make it. I really will."

✳✳✳✳✳

I interviewed three people to take Pat's place. I finally decided to hire Helga Jorgenson, a local resident. Helga was in her fifties, and a widow. She was the Motherly type and took a genuine interest in me and the tearoom. She headed up the Sunday school at the Baptist church, and was quite well known for the strudels she made every Christmas. I was sure her culinary skills would be a real asset to the tea room. Best yet, since she was not presently employed, she could start immediately. It would be wonderful to have steady help in the kitchen again, and Marcie would be so relieved.

Late in the afternoon, Jimmie, the delivery boy from the florist, came by. I was surprised to see him, since he'd already delivered the flowers for the tables earlier in the day.

"These are for you," he grinned, as he handed me a beautiful bouquet of mixed flowers.

"Who would send me flowers?" I opened the card, while Marcie and Jimmie looked on, waiting for the answer.

"Hope you'll let me take you to lunch one day, soon." It was signed "Frank".

Lunch. Didn't the man understand that I had a tea room to run? But, still, it was pretty special to get flowers! Very good for my ego.

✳✳✳✳✳

I left the shop shortly before four and headed down the old gravel road to the Harwood Mansion. I parked my car in a clearing at the end of the road, but still some distance from the house. I wanted to let Liz and her "prospect" have an unobstructed view of the front of the building as they drove up. The big white pillars always reminded me of a Southern plantation.

Although it was early spring, the bare branches of the many trees on the property were already beginning to sprout foliage producing buds. The limbs, heavy with new life, moved slowly in the gusty wind. Dark clouds raced silently across the sky. The mansion, covered in shadows, dared me to come closer.

I sat in the car wishing I had not come alone. I looked at my inexpensive, but serviceable, watch. Liz was late again. My thoughts soon turned to Bob and Frank. The two men were so different. Bob was obviously a working man, struggling to build a business. He was a widower, and quite bitter about the loss of his wife. I really didn't know much more about him.

Frank was rich, respected, and secure in who he was. Other than that, I didn't know much about him, either. Both were handsome men, though Frank was much older. And I had to admit, I was attracted to both men. But, was it Frank or his money I was attracted to?

I glanced again at my watch. I was tired of waiting. I got out of the car. The slam of my own car door broke the silence, and startled me. I wished Liz would get here.

I started walking down to the house. A shiver of fear swept down my spine when I saw there was a man standing on the front porch, watching me! Darn these contact lenses. I meant to get new ones last week. They were just foggy enough that I couldn't see clearly who it was. I squinted. Maybe it was – yes, it was! Bob. He stepped off the porch and started walking towards me. I was so relieved; I wanted to run into his arms, just like they do in the movies. I restrained myself. With my luck, I'd trip and fall flat on my face.

"I thought I heard a car door," he said. "What a nice surprise. What are you doing out here?"

"I'm supposed to meet Liz. She's showing the place to some prospects." I added, as an afterthought, "Are you the prospect?"

"No, not me," he laughed. "I can't afford a place like this. It would take a fortune to restore."

He took my arm and helped me around some debris in our path. "I've heard so much about this old place, I just wanted to come out and take a good look for myself. I got rained out the last time I was here. Remember?"

As if I could forget!

"Come around the side, and let me show you something." He guided me around the side of the old mansion. We climbed up the steps to the side porch. "First, notice the carvings on the railings and over the doorways. There are carvings of magnolia flowers, in the trim, all over the house. Every window and door overhang has them."

His hand lovingly followed the carvings of the flower in the ornate door. "And just look at this stained glass window. This is the work of a real craftsman." He held back a loose board covering a window, revealing part of a stained glass panel.

"I wish we could see the inside," I said, trying to peer through one of the panes.

"I venture to say the magnolia theme is carried out on the interior trim, too," he said.

Our heads touched, as together we looked through the opening. I didn't pull away. Neither did he.

"Emily," he finally said. He straightened up, and I felt small and safe next to him. He took my hand. "There's so much you don't know about me."

I looked into his troubled eyes. "Do you want to tell me?"

"Yes. Someday, maybe." The moment was gone. He seemed to pull a shield over himself. "I'm sorry about the turn our conversation took the other night. I didn't mean to tell you I was angry at God."

"God knows all about your anger anyway, so it's alright to talk about it," I assured him.

"I suppose he does. Hadn't thought of it that way," he admitted.

"Were you in church Sunday, by any chance?" I decided to risk asking him.

"No. I missed it. I'm afraid I'm not in the habit of regular attendance, you know?"

"Pastor Steve talked about forgiveness. I was kind of hoping you were there. He explained some things." I stole a glance at him. Dare I say more?

"It would take a miracle for me to be able to forgive the drunk driver that hit Carol." The muscles in his jaw tightened.

"I still believe in miracles," I said softly. *Lord, help me say the right thing.*

"When I see one, I'll believe." He looked up at the dark, threatening sky. "Don't know if I've ever seen one."

We stepped off the porch and began walking to the front of the house.

He glanced at his watch. "Doesn't look like Liz is going to show up. Her prospect must have cancelled."

"I guess I'll never get to see the inside of this old place," I said. I stuffed my hands into my jacket pocket in resignation.

"Come on, I'll walk you to your car. If we're not careful, we're going to get stuck in another rain storm." He smiled. "In a way, I'm glad Liz didn't make it. It gave us a chance to talk."

He opened the car door for me. I love the way his eyes crinkle up when he smiles. I had to say something, or I would melt right there and then.

"By the way, did you know Arthur is selling his shop?" What a dumb thing to say at such a tender moment. But, that's me, all babbles and bumbles.

"He is? No, I didn't know that." Bob looked surprised. "The last time I saw him, he was bragging about how great his business was doing. Hmm, I better get busy and get that old chair of his put together." Big rain drops began to fall, as he closed my car door and sprinted towards his.

I drove away wondering what would prompt Arthur to sell his business when it was doing so well?

Chapter 16

I drove by Liz's office to see if her car was there. I was surprised to see that it still was. It looked like most of the other staff had already left for the day. I parked in one of the empty spaces.

She was on the phone when I entered. She motioned for me to sit down. I plunked down in a leather chair across from her desk. Finally, she hung up the phone and turned to me.

"Where were you at four o'clock?" I demanded.

"I tried to reach you as soon as my prospect cancelled," she defended herself. She stuffed papers into a file folder.

"When was that?" I dug in my purse for my cell phone.

"Well, it was sort of last minute," she admitted as she waved a fuchsia painted fingernail at me. "Is your cell phone turned off again?"

"I keep forgetting to charge the darn thing," I confessed. I took it out of my purse and punched a button. The low battery message appeared.

"No wonder I couldn't get you." She stopped fiddling with papers and file folders. She leaned forward, a worried look on her face. "You didn't go out there, did you?"

"Yes, but it turned out OK." I proceeded to tell her all about meeting Bob there. I just finished recounting our conversation when I heard a noise at the door and turned to see who it was. Bear's burly frame completely filled the doorway.

"Hello, ladies. Care to tell me why your car was seen out at the Harwood place, Emily? Weren't plannin' on another break in, were ya?" He reeked of garlic. Either he'd just been eating or he'd been to one of Jean's sales meetings and was now taking a garlic supplement she'd sold him. My guess was spaghetti and garlic bread, based on the red stain on his tie.

"Come on in, Bear," Liz cheerily invited. "No more break-ins, we promise! Em was supposed to meet me, and a client, out there, but the client cancelled." She pointed to a chair for him to sit in.

"Dead cell phone," I said, dangling it before him. "She couldn't reach me to tell me she wasn't coming, so I went out there anyway." Should I tell him Bob was there? Or did he already know that too?

"It's a good thing you're here, Bear. Em has something to tell you." Liz nodded to me, as if encouraging me.

"I do?" My mind was blank. Well, not really. It was still full of romantic thoughts of Bob.

"Tell him about Sammy," Liz instructed.

"Bear sat up, at full attention. At least, as much as his round tummy would allow. "What about Sammy?"

"He paid Em a visit and threatened her," Liz exclaimed. Leave it to her to steal my thunder.

Bear took out a small notebook from his back pocket. "Maybe you better tell me all about that," and then he added, "and anything else you've been up to."

Funny how things will jog your memory. All of a sudden, I remembered the button I'd found days ago. It was still in my jacket pocket. I hadn't even told Liz about it.

"Uh, well, I guess there is something else. Probably doesn't mean a thing, that's why I forgot all about it. Um, well, the thing is, I, uh, I found a button out at the Harwood mansion several days ago. It was kind of buried in the leaves."

"With-holding evidence!" Bear growled. "Where is it? I want to see it."

I sheepishly dug in my pocket, and presented it to him.

"You never told me you found a button!" Liz complained. She came around her desk to get a better look at the button.

Bear questioned me some more about finding the button, and when he was satisfied that I wasn't deliberately sabotaging the case, he relaxed. "Now, what's this about Sammy threatening you?"

I told him, word for word, best as I could remember, exactly what happened when Sammy visited me.

"Then what happened?" he asked as I ended my story.

"Well, then Arthur came right over. He said he saw a man running out of my shop and wanted to be sure I was alright." I told Bear, word for word, our conversation and that Arthur referred to Sammy by name even though I hadn't mentioned his name.

I could see the same question forming in his mind that had bothered Liz and me. He continued scribbling in his notepad.

"Well, I just hope Emily's next new neighbor will be as caring as Arthur," Liz said as she twirled a jewel encrusted letter opener in the air, waiting for a reaction from Bear. There wasn't any. "You know, after Arthur sells his place," she added nonchalantly.

That did it. "Arthur's selling his shop? Since when?" Bear stopped writing and stared at Liz.

Liz leaned forward, happy to be the center of attention again. "Since last night. He listed it with a realtor in Westport. The traitor."

Bear looked puzzled. "Wonder why he'd do that. I'd think he'd list with the best realtor around these parts. And that would be you, Liz."

"Well, I made a few phone calls and I found out something else pretty strange," she said. "He doesn't want his business advertised in this area, or put up on multiple listing boards. It's almost like he wants to keep the news that he's selling a secret." She frowned. "Pretty darn hard to sell a property if you can't list it, or advertise it."

"Sounds impossible to me," I agreed.

"No, it's possible, just more difficult. You have to advertise it out of the county or state. I've done it a couple of times," she bragged.

Bear shifted his weight in the simple office chair that was not designed for heavy weights. "Guess I'll have to stop by Arthur's shop tomorrow, myself. Course, there's no law saying a man can't sell his business any way he wants to." He looked at Liz. "Or through any realtor he chooses."

"Of course not," Liz agreed. "It's just a strange way to do business, that's all."

After Bear left, I headed for home. I'd forgotten to tell Liz about the flowers from Frank, but with the connections she had all over town, she probably knew all about them anyway.

After a gourmet meal of frozen food, I put in a load of laundry, and sat down at my computer to catch up on some personal bill paying. A few clicks and the gas and electric bill, and cell phone service were all paid for. That reminded me to plug in my cell phone and recharge it. Funny how things work out. If my cell phone had been working, Liz would have reached me in time to tell me her client had cancelled, and I would not have gone out to the Harwood place. I wouldn't have met Bob there again. *Lord, thank you for caring about the smallest details of my life. You are in control of all things.*

The phone rang and I wondered what Liz was calling about now. But it wasn't Liz. I recognized the smooth voice immediately. "Good evening, Emily. I hope I'm not disturbing you."

"No, Frank, not at all. Thank you for the flowers. They are just beautiful."

"You know the old saying, 'Beautiful flowers for a beautiful lady.' I'm glad you liked them. I hoped they might brighten your day. You've been through so much lately." He sounded sincerely sympathetic.

"Yes, they were the bright spot of the day," I said. But they weren't, really. Being with Bob still took first place.

"I wondered when we might get together for that lunch date?" he inquired.

"Well," I hesitated. Crumpet meowed for attention. "There is a slight problem."

"Not one that can't be fixed, I hope," he said.

"I'd love to have lunch with you, but there's the tea room, you see. Lunch hour is my busiest time, and I just can't get away then."

"Oh," There was disappointment in his voice.

"Except for Sundays, "I offered. "But I can't make it this Sunday either." I'd promised to attend Marcie's birthday party. She was turning forty, and not too happy about it.

"A week from Sunday, then? But that's so far away," he said. "I was hoping we could get together sooner."

"I'm sorry," was all I could think of to say.

"I've got it!" he said. "We'll just make it dinner instead of lunch. How about tomorrow evening? Are you free?"

It all happened so fast; the change from lunch to dinner. It seemed the perfect solution, and yet after the details had been settled and we hung up, I was apprehensive. Lunch is so harmless. It's daytime, it's more businesslike. Dinner is more like a real date, with romantic undertones. It's more intimate, and intimidating. So why was I smiling?

✳✳✳✳✳

It was great having Helga at the tea room. She just fit right in and picked up on things immediately. New delights came out of the oven and filled the showcases. She had a light hand with sauces and brought new recipes for

Scandinavian tarts and cream filled pastries. *Thank you, Lord.* "My God will meet all your needs, according to his glorious riches in Christ Jesus." (Phil 4:19 NIV) Surely God had sent Helga.

When I came back from the post office, Marcie giggled as she gave me a phone message.

"Here, you better check on this one right away. Helga answered the phone, while I was waiting on customers, and took this message for you."

I stared at the memo pad in disbelief. "Call 672-4253. In the subject line was hand written the words "birth control."

Marcie grinned. "Got a new boyfriend, huh?"

I marched back to Helga. "Helga, what's this phone message all about?"

She looked perfectly innocent, with her long blond hair in one braid, falling down her back. She brushed a stray curl away from her face. "Yah, that' what the lady said. She wants for you to call her, to talk about birth control," she said in her sing-song Norwegian voice.

If this was one of Liz's jokes, she'd gone too far! Birth control, because I had two men in my life. Just wait till I get my hands on her!

"I'll see what this is all about," I said, angrily punching the number into my cell phone. Helga and Marcie waited in suspense.

"Wilson's Pest Control," a woman's voice answered.

"Pest Control?" I echoed loudly enough for them to hear. "Yes, is it time for our quarterly service again?"

Helga shrugged her shoulders and turned away. "Yah, I knew it was something like that. Pest control, birth control, what's the difference?"

Marcie collapsed laughing.

What a way to start the day. I hoped Arthur would come in for lunch, so I could question him about selling his shop. I wondered if he would tell me, or if I would have to bring up the subject. After the lunch rush hour was over, I couldn't be patient any longer. I decided to pay him a visit.

A bell jangled as I opened the door to Arthur's shop. He came out from the back room, with a pleasant smile on his face, expecting to see a customer. He was busily wiping his stain covered hands on a rag. He must have been working with some sort of varnish, refinishing an antique, or something. There was a chemical smell in the air. He did a fast double take when he discovered it was just me.

"Oh, it's you, Emily. What brings you over? Have you heard the news already, too?"

"News? What news?" I tried to sound innocent. Apparently, it didn't work.

"Don't be coy with me. If Bear knows, then the whole town must know."

I guessed that Bear had lost no time in talking to Arthur. "Well, yes, I did hear something about you selling the business. Is it true then?" I looked around the shop. There were so many things to admire.

Arthur sat down on an antique love seat, upholstered in dark red velvet. He patted the seat next to him for me to sit down, too. I pretended I didn't notice his suggestion and picked up a small vase to examine, while I waited for his answer.

"I have no choice, due to some circumstances beyond my control. It's, uh, a family matter."

"Is it Sue? Is she sick?" I became alarmed.

"Oh, she's fine." He hesitated. "It's her mother. She's become very ill, and we need to move there, to take care of her. It's all been very sudden."

"What a shame," I said. "You've worked so hard to build up this business."

"Yes, it's very – unfortunate. I wasn't expecting anything like this." He adjusted his tie.

"Where does her mother live? Isn't there any other way? Any other relatives?" It seemed like such a drastic move to make so suddenly.

"She lives in Arkansas." He shook his head. "No, there's no other way. In fact, Sue's already gone. I sent her off yesterday."

"And the business; you've already listed it?" It was more of a statement than a question.

"I hope Liz won't be offended." He examined his hands. "I listed it with another realtor, because I was trying to keep the sale under cover, so to speak. You know how people are, once they find out the business is for sale, they stop coming in. So, I didn't want it to be common knowledge in Riverbend. But I guess it is, after all." He looked genuinely distressed.

"I'm afraid so," I agreed. "You said Bear came in to talk to you?"

"Yes," I don't know how he found out so quickly. He wanted to know my reason for selling. Rather odd, I thought. And he asked me about you, too."

"Me?" I was dumbfounded. Why would Bear ask Arthur anything about me?

"Yes. He said he wanted to know about the day Sammy made a visit to your shop." He turned and walked over to the window. "He wanted to know all about it, what state of mind you were in when I found you, what you said and… things like that."

"I see. What did you tell him?"

"I told him the truth. You were shaking and holding a knife."

"I was holding a knife? I don't remember that." I truly didn't.

"Don't you? I assumed that's how you scared Sammy into leaving. Anyway, that's what I told Bear."

Great. Now Bear thinks I'm a knife-wielding psycho.

"Well, somehow I got rid of him. I thank the Lord for his protection that day."

"I never did understand why Sammy wanted to threaten you. Do you know something about Pat's murder, Emily?" His eyes narrowed and I didn't like the way he looked at me.

"What could I know? I, uh, I guess Sammy thought Pat might have told me something about an argument I'd overheard between him and Pat, and I'd go to the police. But she never told me anything. You know Pat. She wasn't one to share her private life with anyone."

Arthur frowned. "You're probably the closest thing to a friend she ever had, though." He took a step forward and smiled.

A warning bell went off in my brain. "Well, I better get back to the tearoom. Good luck with selling your shop." I hurried back to the safety of my precious tearoom.

I opened the door to find Liz sitting at a tea table, waiting for me. "Well, what did you find out?"

I told her everything, especially that he said I was holding the knife.

"Why would he say something like that to Bear?"

"I suppose he was trying to get attention off himself and onto you. Remember the body they found out at the Harwood place? That guy had been stabbed." She bit into an orange-anise muffin.

I shuddered. "You don't think Bear thinks…"

"Of course not." She looked thoughtful and then changed the subject, again. "Doesn't Sue's mother live in Pennsylvania?"

I tried to remember. Something about Pennsylvania Dutch came to my mind. "Yes, I think she does. I remember Sue saying how her Mom was trying to get some local artists to send some of their crafts to Arthur."

"Yes! And he didn't want anything to do with them. Too folksy, not the image he wanted to build," she said, with triumph, as she recalled it.

"Well, he said it was all very sudden. Maybe her Mom moved to Arkansas suddenly, too." I sat down, thinking a cup of Earl Grey tea would taste very good right now, with a muffin.

"Sure," Liz mocked. "I'm sure it's the dream of every Pennsylvanian to retire to Arkansas."

The phone rang. It was Bear. He "invited" me down to see Sheriff Doyle, just as soon as I could. I left Helga to finish cleaning and close up, and Liz accompanied me to the Sheriff's office.

Sheriff Doyle greeted us very cordially, though he didn't bother to remove the toothpick from his mouth. He thanked me for turning in the button and said it had been dusted for prints. Of course, mine were the only ones on it. He asked a few more questions, but I could see he wasn't very interested in the button. Then he leaned back in his chair, still chewing on the toothpick, and asked me to tell him all about my visit from Sammy.

"You say Sammy picked up a knife from the table while he talked to you. What did he do with that knife?"

"He just kind of stroked the blade while he told me not to go to the police with the story of their argument."

"And when you threatened to scream?" It fascinated me how he could talk with a toothpick stuck between his lips.

"He dropped it on the floor and ran out, as if he'd seen a ghost," I answered proudly.

"And what did you do?" He folded his hands over his stomach and waited while I thought back to those terrifying moments.

"I watched him run down the street and around the corner. I remember thinking his truck wasn't parked anywhere nearby. Then I collapsed in a chair," I admitted sheepishly.

"You didn't pick up the knife?" He leaned forward, looking directly at me.

I remembered clearly now. "No. Arthur came over to see what was going on. He said he saw a man running away from my shop, and was concerned about me. When Arthur left, I locked the door, and walked back into the work room. My foot accidently kicked the knife, and that's when I picked it up. I put it in the dishwasher."

"You're sure that's just the way everything happened?" he shifted the toothpick to the other side of his mouth. I nodded.

The Sheriff went on. "Well, we've been trying to find Sammy to ask him a few questions. He seems to have disappeared. Cleared out of the room he was renting, and Trina says she doesn't know where he is, either. Looked like she'd been crying a lot."

"Sheriff, do you have a way to find out where someone lives?" Liz asked. "You see," Liz was just warming up to her request, "Arthur says he's selling his business because Sue's mother in Arkansas is very sick, and they have to go take care of her. But we remember that Sue's mother lives in Pennsylvania." She was on a roll, now. "Of course, it could be she moved there recently, or it could be that Arthur is lying about his reason for selling. If that's the case, I wonder why, don't you?" She actually batted her eyelashes at him, trying to look innocent.

"Guess it wouldn't hurt to check that out." He nodded to Bear.

Murder at the Fancy Frills Tea Room

Sheriff Doyle stood up. His leather belt and holster made a creaking noise. "Thanks for coming down, ladies." He looked at me. "You be careful, Emily, you hear?"

✶✶✶✶✶

Liz tried, again, to talk me into moving in with her and Roger till this whole thing was over, but I still didn't want to do that. She was very persistent.

I had to change the subject so I told her that I was going out with Frank that very evening, and wanted to hurry home and get ready. She was delighted, and began offering fashion advice.

It was hard to put all the events of the past few days aside, and focus once more on my own private life. I wished my date was with Bob instead of Frank. How could I help Bob to understand his bitterness was hurting him more than the man responsible for his wife's death. He needed to understand God's love and put it into practice in his own life. It would surely take a miracle. *Lord, you are the God of miracles. I pray you will help Bob forgive that drunk driver, and find peace.*

✶✶✶✶✶

Frank arrived right on time. He wore a dark suit that brought out the highlights in his silver hair. He looked very handsome. I felt proud to be seen with him, and held my head high as he escorted me into the most expensive restaurant in the area. I knew I was the envy of every woman in the place as we were led to our table. It was already set with fresh flowers and champagne. I was about to protest the bubbly, but before I had a chance, the cork was popped and the amber liquid was swirling about in my glass.

Oh, well, a little won't hurt me. Actually, I was glad I had some. It helped me relax, and when Frank asked me to dance, I felt light as a feather in his arms.

He twirled me about the floor, and I had to admit it was fun. He held me just close enough that our bodies brushed against each other as we swayed to the music. I was glad he didn't crush me against him like some of the jerks Liz had set me up with. No wonder they call those guys 'mashers.'

We returned to our table, warm and thirsty. The champagne tasted even better now. This was fun! Here I was, at an expensive restaurant, seated across from an affluent, handsome man. Who could want more?

Frank pushed a small, velvet box across the table. "I hope I'm not rushing things, but when I saw this, I just had to get it for you. I hope you don't mind."

I gasped as I opened the box. It was a beautiful cameo on a gold chain. "It's beautiful, Frank, but I can't – I mean, I hardly know you. This is much too expensive. I can't possibly accept it." I pushed it back across the table.

"Please, Emily. It would mean so much to me for you to accept it." He pushed it towards me, again.

""But, Frank, I –"

"I have no one to give gifts to, and I love giving. Please make me happy by accepting it. Think of it as an early birthday present." He looked a little sad as he withdrew his hand from the box.

"Well, I, uh -" I lifted the cameo out of the box to examine it closer. It was beautifully set in gold filigree.

Murder at the Fancy Frills Tea Room

"When is your birthday?" He looked hopeful.

I put it back. "Not until November."

"Then, Happy Birthday, my dear."

The waiter brought our dinners just then. He smiled at me. "Happy Birthday, Madam." He filled my glass with champagne again.

Frank lifted his glass and smiled.

What could I do? I was clearly outnumbered. "I don't know what to say, "I mumbled. I felt confused. I didn't want to hurt his feelings, he looked so happy.

"It's the most beautiful piece of jewelry I've ever seen. I'll think of you every time I wear it," I smiled back at him.

"Then I hope you'll wear it every day." We clicked our glasses together, and once more the champagne slid down my throat. I wasn't feeling any effect of the champagne at all, and was surprised at how well I could handle alcohol.

Frank told me about his life, and how lonely he was. I could certainly relate to loneliness. Maybe that's why I felt so comfortable with him.

The evening passed in a swirl of champagne, dinner, dancing and talking. I had a wonderful time. If this was life in the fast track, let the race begin!

Chapter 17

My head was throbbing. I opened my eyes and the sunlight was blinding. My mouth felt dry and full of cotton balls. What was wrong with me? Then I remembered. Champagne. How much did I have to drink last night, anyway?

Last night. Memories of dancing, dinner and a cameo came rushing to my mind. Cameo. Did I dream that, or had it really happened? I stumbled out of bed, and there on my dresser was the cameo. It was real all right.

I splashed cold water on my face and tried to remember what happened after dinner. More dancing. More champagne. I groaned. Lots of talk. I remembered Frank's pleasant smile, perfect teeth, and his talking about being lonely and needing someone special in his life.

I had intended to talk to him about the Lord, and find out what his beliefs were, but somehow I never got around to that. Did it really matter that much? I mean, couldn't I have a relationship with a rich man and still keep my beliefs? Maybe I could even lead him to the Lord. Maybe that's why God brought him into my life. A red flag went up in my conscience, but I ignored it.

Somehow I managed to get to the tea room on time. I was thankful it was a slow day, and both Marcy and Helga were there to take care of business.

Murder at the Fancy Frills Tea Room

Liz came bouncing through the door around two o'clock. She was dressed in a lavender suit with a fuchsia blouse. A bright yellow scarf was tied in a big bow under her chin. Lilac painted toenails peeked out of her yellow high heel sandals.

"You look like an Easter Egg," I said in greeting.

"Well, aren't you the perky one," she said as she peered at me. "It's spring, remember? Don't you feel well, honey?"

"I'm fine," I lied. "Just a little tired."

"Ooo, that's right," she squealed. "You were out with Frank last night. Tell, tell, tell!" She plopped down in a chair.

I crumpled into the chair next to hers. "It was, uh, well, uh, it was, it was nice."

"Nice? Coming from you that means it was pretty terrific." She helped herself to a blueberry scone.

I smiled at the memory and added, "We went to the Paragon." Caffeine. That's what I need. Lots and lots of caffeine.

She slathered lemon curd on the scone, and topped it off with a generous dab of Devonshire cream. "The Paragon? Wow! He must have really wanted to impress you. Then what happened?"

"Well, we had champagne, and danced, and we had dinner, and danced some more." Watching her eat the scone with lemon curd and cream was causing my tummy to do funny flip flops.

Maxine Holmgren

"I can't believe my baby sister had champagne and danced with a man! I think I'm gonna cry!" She wiped a crumb from her mouth.

"You cry at super market openings." I paused. "There's more. He gave me a beautiful cameo pendant for my birthday."

"Now I know I'm gonna cry." The scone stopped half way to her mouth. "Wait a minute. Your birthday's not till November."

"I know," I gloated. "It's an early gift." I poured myself a big mug of coffee. Thank goodness, Helga makes it strong.

She put the scone down and touched my arm. "I'm so excited for you."

"Well, don't get too excited. I don't know anything about his faith, yet."

"Oh, well, you can always convert him. Isn't that what us Christians are always trying to do, anyway? May as well be a rich convert as a poor one, I always say."

The door opened and Jean burst through the door. She wore a big button that read "Ask me how to eat and lose weight!"

"Hi, Emily and Liz! How are you?"

I fell for the trap by automatically responding, "Fine. How are you?"

"I'm getting richer every day," she proudly answered. "And you can too! I just set up an impromptu meeting with some people later this afternoon and I need some dessert to serve. I hope you can come, too! You could sell this amazing new product here in your store and become a millionaire!" She said it all in one breath.

Liz conveniently remembered a phone call she had to make and excused herself, leaving me to fend for myself. I made excuses and helped Jean pick out a dessert.

She was still telling me the incredible benefits of her ground-breaking opportunity, as I walked her to the door. I was careful to put up the closed sign after she finally left.

Liz kicked off her shoes, hung her suit jacket up carefully, and pitched in to help me clean up and close up for the day. I was glad she did. The aspirin I'd taken earlier was starting to wear off, and my energy was at low ebb. It was a relief to finally lock the door.

"By the way, have you talked with Bob lately?" Liz inquired as she swept the floor. "I ran in to him at the coffee shop, and we were having a nice conversation over coffee, when all of a sudden, he rushed off to some important appointment. At seven o'clock in the evening." She stopped sweeping and looked at me. "I thought maybe it was a date with you?"

"No, not me." The green monster flared up within me. Who was Bob's important date? And why should I care, anyway? But I did.

*****

I turned down Liz's invitation to spend the evening with them, and decided a walk in the park would be just the thing to clear my head. The lilacs were blooming down the street and the aroma filled the air. I drove to the park, and parked my car in the empty lot. I didn't see the truck that pulled in shortly after me. I headed down the path, enjoying the bright yellow daffodils and red tulips. I wished I had planted more daffodils in my front yard. The first harbingers of spring, they always were so bright and cheerful.

"Emily!" a voice shouted.

I turned to see Bob hurrying towards me.

"I thought that was your car in the parking lot. May I join you?" He looked masculine and handsome in jeans and a denim jacket.

"Sure. It's such a pleasant afternoon, I thought I'd take advantage of it and go for a walk."

"Any new developments?" he asked as he matched my stride.

It took me a minute to realize he was asking about the murder case, not my love life. "Well, the Sheriff called me in for questioning."

He looked alarmed. "But, why you?"

I brought him up to date and said, "It seems Arthur told him that when he came into the shop, I was holding a knife. He assumed that's how I scared Sammy away."

Bob stopped in his tracks. "Were you?"

I turned to him. "No, of course not. But he said I was shaking and had the knife in my hands. It's true I was shaking all right, but I wasn't holding the knife. Actually it had dropped to the floor, and I stepped on it later. That's when I picked it up. I put it in the dishwasher."

"Why would Arthur tell the Sheriff a story like that?" Bob asked. We followed the path that ran along the river.

Murder at the Fancy Frills Tea Room

"That's not all. Arthur says his wife has to take care of her mother in Arkansas, but Liz and I are pretty sure her Mother lives in Pennsylvania. Of course, she could have moved. The Sheriff is going to check it out."

"Strange," he agreed. "And you?" He reached for my hand. "How are you doing through all this?"

"I'm all right. A little nervous, maybe, but I'm trusting the Lord through it all." His hand was wrapped around mine. My heart was beating so loud I was sure he could hear it.

"I want you to know, I'm here for you, anytime you want to talk – or need anything." We stood inches apart, looking at each other. My knees felt weak, as I gazed into those dreamy dark eyes.

"There something I want you to know. Pastor Steve said I should tell you." He looked very serious and led me to a bench. We sat silently for a moment.

Here it comes. He's leaving town. He's dying of an incurable disease. He's wanted in five states for armed robbery. My mind flew into an abyss of despair.

"It's about Carol," he continued. "After she was killed by that drunk driver, I kind of hit bottom. I started drinking, and I didn't stop. I couldn't stop. I just wanted to drown out all the grief and pain I was feeling, and alcohol was the only way I could escape the pain. Can you understand that?"

I nodded. He wasn't dying? It was something else. I told my mind to pay attention.

He went on. "I'm ashamed to tell you this," He looked away for what seemed like an eternity. "It got so bad, I'd go

Maxine Holmgren

on benders that lasted for weeks. Eventually, it cost me everything I'd worked so hard for. I lost my business, my home, my reputation. And it didn't seem to matter, because Carol was gone, too."

"But, you're fine now – "I started to say.

"Yes, now." He didn't let me finish my sentence. "For the last twelve months I've been sober. But, I had to hit rock bottom before I came to my senses. I finally came to realize that Carol wouldn't like what I was doing. I had to change before I killed myself, or someone else, just like that drunk driver that killed her. Believe it or not, sometimes I would drive after I'd been drinking." He looked across the river, and I could tell he was reliving a memory.

"It wasn't till I had a minor accident, that I came to my senses. I hit a tree, but it could have been another car, or a person. It really scared me. So, to make a long story short, I joined AA, got a job, and slowly started rebuilding my life and my business. I still go to AA meetings, probably always will." He took a deep breath. "I go to the meetings in Westport because I didn't want anyone here in Riverbend to know my history."

"I'm glad you told me," I reassured him. "But I'm puzzled. Why did Pastor Steve want you to tell me?"

He put his arm around me and looked into my eyes. "Because I've come to care for you very much, and he said you had a right to know." He paused. "I was afraid I'd lose you if you knew the truth, but I couldn't deceive you. He said I could trust you; that you would understand. Do you, Emily? Or does it make a difference?"

I was elated. "Oh, Bob, the only difference it makes is that I'm even more proud of you, now that I know what you've been through; what you've conquered. Only the power of God could have brought about such a change in you. Now, I know you really do believe in God."

It was like a dark cloud passed over us. When would I learn to keep my big mouth shut and quit while I was ahead?

"AA teaches us to have faith in a higher force than ourselves, Emily, that's true. But I'm not sure it's this God you're always talking about." He turned away, his arm dropping from my shoulder. "It's like he's a real person to you. I believe in a higher being, but I've never met this God you talk about." His voice turned cold. "I told you once I didn't believe in miracles, and I still don't. I believe in hard work, and making right decisions. I believe in AA."

I didn't know what to say. I wanted to back up the conversation to the part where he said he cared about me. I didn't want to get into a theological argument.

"Look," he said, "I don't want to get into a big discussion. I just want to let you know where I'm coming from. I care about you. I can't stop thinking about you, Emily. I'd like to spend more time with you, so we can get to know each other better. How does that sound to you?"

"It sounds wonderful," I eagerly answered. I could tell him more about God later.

He gathered me in his arms and kissed me. His kiss was light and tender, with the promise of more.

We held hands as we walked back to our cars. He walked, I floated.

✳✳✳✳✳

Crumpet was glad to see me come home. She meowed profusely and followed me everywhere. I fixed her dinner and watched her eat as I ate mine. I was too tired to cook, so I had picked up a small pizza before I came home.

The clouds that had threatened rain in the afternoon, delivered in the evening. I changed into comfortable pajamas and wrapped my robe around me. My favorite mindless sitcom was on, and it kept me company as I tried to sort out all that had been happening lately. Where had that boring, dull, routine life I used to have, disappear to? Now my days were filled with murder, mystery, suspicion, and yes, even romance!

The security alarm shrieked the same moment there was a crash in the kitchen. It doesn't make sense to rush into a room where that has just happened, but that's what I did. Reflexes, I guess. The kitchen window was shattered and a large rock lay on the kitchen floor. There was an envelope tied to it. I picked my way through the broken glass and picked it up. My hands were shaking so hard, I could hardly open it. "Keep your mouth shut. Mind your own business. Or else you're next." The words were written in an ugly, black scrawl.

I was frozen to the spot. I knew I should call the police, but I couldn't seem to move. This couldn't be happening. This was unreal. Things like this just don't take place in real life; not here in Riverbend.

Slowly, other sounds filtered through to my numb mind. The neighbor's dog was barking. In the distance I could hear a police siren. It was getting closer and closer. Soon there was pounding on the door.

Murder at the Fancy Frills Tea Room

"Emily! Are you in there? Open up! It's Bear."

I stepped carefully around the pieces of glass and opened the door.

Bear rushed in. "Are you alright? What happened?" Then he saw the broken window and the rock. I still held the note in my hand.

"What's that?" he said as he took the note from my hand. "Was that attached to the rock?"

I could only nod.

"Let me see." He read the threatening words. "Who did this, Emily? What are you supposed to keep your mouth shut about? What do they mean, mind your own business?"

"I don't know," I stammered. "I mean, I've told you everything I heard, even about Arthur selling and his wife going to Arkansas instead of Pennsylvania and – what should I do?" Suddenly I felt helpless and very vulnerable. I scooped up Crumpet and held her close.

Bear punched some numbers in the alarm system and it stopped as suddenly as it had begun. The silence seemed almost as deafening; spooky, somehow.

"You got somewhere to go for the night? I'll get that window closed up temporarily, till you can get it fixed proper." He put the note in his pocket.

"I'll call Liz and tell her I'm coming over."

"You might want to stay there 'till we get this settled. Doesn't seem safe for you here." He glanced around the room.

I couldn't have agreed with him more. I called Liz and gathered some things together while Bear checked the outside of the house, looking for clues. Liz took pity on me and even said I could bring Crumpet.

"I'll follow you over to Liz's, just to make sure nothing else happens," Bear offered.

I was grateful for his concern. The rain had let up, but the wind had grown stronger. The trees cast strange moving shadows in the reflection of the street lights.

Liz and Roger stood in the open doorway of their home, waiting for me. Worry was written on their faces.

"Good thing you let me have that security system put in your house, "Liz crowed. "Are you all right, honey?"

"Thanks for letting me come." It felt good to be in their home. Safe.

"Shouldn't be any more trouble," Bear told Roger. "Somebody just tryin' to scare her. We'll find out who and get to the bottom of this. Till then, might be best if Emily wasn't alone."

"Thanks for your help, Bear." Roger shook Bear's big hand. "We'll take good care of her. Any luck in finding that Sammy character?"

"Not yet, but don't worry. We'll find him. He's got a record a mile long, you know."

"No, we didn't know," Liz grabbed his arm. "What kind of record?"

"He was in the state pen for armed robbery, assault, drugs, you name it, and he's done it. He's been out just about long enough to get involved in another scheme." He hitched up his pants.

Something clicked inside my befuddled head. "Bear, wasn't that Johnson guy – you know, the body they found at the mansion – didn't he serve time, too? Was it at the same prison?"

"As a matter of fact, it was. We're checking into that, too. They might have known each other." He tipped his hat to us. "Well, gotta go. You'll be alright now, Emily. Try to get some sleep, all of you."

We watched Bear drive away in the squad car, each of us lost in our own thoughts.

"How about some tea, everybody? It's just what we need to help us wind down. I've got scones, too. I brought some peanut butter and chocolate chip scones home from the tea shop today. I can't resist them," Liz said as she headed for the kitchen. Roger put his arm around me, and we followed her billowing purple caftan down the hall.

*****

I stayed with Liz and Roger for the next week. The time passed quickly and quietly. There was no more news about Sammy's whereabouts, and no new developments in the two murders.

Frank was out of town on business, but he called me at the tea room every day. It was very flattering, as were the flowers and gifts he sent almost daily, too. It would be so easy to be swept away by his attention, but Frank had no interest in God. Every time I tried to bring up the subject of faith, he put up a wall. As a self-made man, he didn't think he needed God.

I was getting tired of his calls, as I was definitely more interested in Bob. I began to let Helga answer the phone and tell him I was busy with customers. She was good at small talk, and didn't seem to mind putting up with all his calls.

Chapter 18

"What is it with men, anyway?" I asked Pastor Steve one day. "Why is it so hard for them to admit they need Jesus in their lives?"

He had taken time out from his busy day to check on me. He also wanted to relax over a cup of apple spice tea and a muffin, and here I was badgering him with questions.

"Did you have anyone in particular in mind, or is that a generic question?" He smiled, knowingly.

"I guess you know." I smiled back. "Bob reminds me of that sausage maker that says "We answer to a higher authority." Why can't he see that his higher force has a name, a personality, is real!" I said in frustration.

"He will, one of these days. I'm sure. Are you praying for him?" He put his chocolate chip muffin down to ask me the question.

"I sure am." I sighed. "Bob keeps saying it will take a miracle."

"Well, our God just happens to be in the miracle business." He took a bite of his muffin and then continued, " I plan on seeing Bob this week. I need to talk to him about having an old pie safe, that Nancy picked up at an estate sale, transformed into an entertainment center. It will take a miracle!" He finished his muffin and looked longingly at the other pastries in the display case.

"She really has an eye for antiques. Well, if anyone can do it, Bob can." I smiled as I thought of him.

"So," he hesitated. "You and Bob. Is it serious?"

Now, it was my turn to hesitate. I felt awkward. "It could be. If only he wasn't so bitter about the past and would ask Jesus to be Lord of his life."

Pastor Steve glanced at the clock, and rose to leave. He patted my hand. "Keep praying, Emily. Don't give up. God isn't finished working in Bob's life. In fact, I have the feeling He's just begun."

✶✶✶✶✶

I was busy making blueberry scones when the phone call came from Bear.

"Emily, we just got word that Trina's been taken to the hospital. Looks like a drug overdose."

"Oh, no! How awful!" I almost dropped the pan of scones. "Is she going to be alright?"

"Hard to tell yet. She had a lot of the stuff in her system." He paused. "Just thought you'd want to know."

"Yes, thanks for telling me. Is she at Westport General?"

"Yes. For now, anyway," he answered.

"Any word on Sammy?" I held my breath, waiting for his answer.

"Not yet, but we're working on it. Trina probably got the drugs from him. If so, that means he's in the area. You take care, now."

"I will." I shuddered. "I remember Pat being worried about Trina. She suspected Trina was on drugs, and blamed it on Sammy."

"Looks like she was right. And look where it got her." He hung up leaving those last words ringing in my ear.

✳✳✳✳✳

I was surprised when Bob called and asked if we could get together that evening. He said he had something to tell me. Was it break off time? Was he going to give me some lame excuse about being too busy to see me anymore? Was he going to confess to the murders? I told myself to stop being paranoid, and trust God. I comforted myself with the thought that God always knows and does what is best for me, because He loves me and wants the best for me. One of my favorite scriptures popped into my head. "Trust in the Lord with all thy heart… and he will make your paths straight." (Prv 3:5,6 NIV) If that 'path' didn't lead to Bob, then so be it. I would continue to trust God. But I sure hoped I was on the right path!

But when we met, Bob was happy and cheerful. Maybe it wouldn't be bad news, after all. We held hands as we walked along the river walk. It was a beautiful warm evening. The setting sun cast a red reflection on the water. I felt God's peace and care as the words of the 23rd Psalm came to my mind. "He leads me beside quiet waters". (Ps23:2 NIV) Surely God had led me to this place, Riverbend, where I had found peace and security. Had he also led Bob into my life?

Murder at the Fancy Frills Tea Room

Bob interrupted my thoughts. "A funny thing happened on the way to the forum". Then he laughed out loud. "Actually, a funny thing happened while I was watching TV today. I was staining a piece of furniture, and I had the tv on in the workroom. This program came on, talking about miracles. A man was telling about his life; how he had been mad about the death of his son. He was mad at God for letting it happen, and mad at the guy who shot his son." He paused, "I wanted to turn off the tv, but I couldn't stop staining the cabinet I was working on. You can't stop the process, once you begin. So I had to listen. Well, he said Jesus came into his life, kind of like a dream or something, and just took away all the anger. He even went so far as to visit the man in jail, who shot his son."

He shook his head in amazement. I was spell bound. I could hardly believe what I was hearing, and hung on every word.

"He was asked how he could forgive his son's murderer, and he said that he realized Jesus forgave those who nailed him to the cross. He figured out that all his anger was only hurting him, and that the only way he would be released was if he forgave, too."

"Yes, that's right." I urged him on.

"Well, I thought about that as I finished spraying the stain. And the more I thought about it, the madder I got!"

My heart sank. That wasn't what I wanted to hear!

"I threw down the sprayer, and shouted at God. "If you're real, show me! Take my anger away, like you did that guy on TV. I don't want to feel like this anymore."

I held my breath. "What happened?"

"It was the darndest thing! I got this warm feeling go all through my body, and an incredible feeling of love. I guess that's what it was. I never felt anything like it before. The next thing I knew, I was on the floor, bawling like a baby. I don't know how long that went on, I just know I was exhausted when I finally stopped. But when it was all over, I felt such peace! Peace like I've never known in all my life. And I wasn't angry anymore. Not angry at God, not even angry at that drunk driver."

"That's wonderful!" I exclaimed. I wiped a tear away from my eyes. Why do I always cry when I'm happy?

We stopped walking and sat down on a bench.

"I didn't know what to make of it all, so I called Pastor Steve. He came right over, and explained a lot of things to me. We prayed together and well, I've got a long way to go, Emily, but I guess I'm what you call a 'believer' now. I believe in Jesus and turned my life over to him."

"That's the best decision you ever made," I said. "I am so happy for you." Now there was nothing standing in the way of a true relationship with Bob. My heart was pounding with joy for him, and for all my dreams, too.

Then he took me in his arms and kissed me. It was a warm, tender kiss and I melted in his arms. I wanted this moment to last forever. Just then some kids on bicycles came riding by, shouting and laughing at us. So much for romance.

Bob laughed, too. He pulled me up and said, "We better go." He kissed me again, and I thought my heart would burst as his lips eagerly sought mine. It was hard to break away, but the kids on bikes were coming back. We started down the walk again, hand in hand.

Finally, he broke the silence. "Remember those chair pieces Arthur brought in?"

I nodded. I really didn't want to talk about Arthur now.

"Well, it was like putting together a jig saw puzzle, but it's back to being a chair again."

"Really? I didn't think there was any hope for that. You really are a genius." I looked up at him with admiration.

"I wouldn't say that, but I am pretty pleased with the result. I just have a few finishing touches, and it will be done," he said.

"Arthur will be so pleased. He can take it with him when he moves." I was still reeling from his kiss, and wanted him to kiss me again, but we walked on.

"Think he'll open another antique store in Arkansas?" he asked. I was surprised how abruptly he changed the subject, but then I realized the kids were still following us on their bikes.

I laughed out loud. "Somehow, I can't even imagine suave, sophisticated Arthur in Arkansas. It's like an oxymoron."

"I wonder how his family is doing. Was it his Mother-in-law that was ill?" Bob picked up a stone and skipped it across the river.

"Uh-huh. I guess we were mistaken about her living in Pennsylvania. Sheriff Doyle was going to look into that. I forgot to ask Bear if they found out anything about it, when he told me about Trina." I tried to skip a stone, too, but mine just went ker-plunk.

We walked on down to the "Cast-a-Net" Restaurant and went inside. Charles, the head waiter, greeted us and seated us at a lovely table, right by the window, overlooking the river. The Delta Queen could be seen downstream. Bob followed my gaze.

"We'll have to do that sometime. I hear the dinner cruise is very nice," he said.

"You must be reading my mind," I laughed. "I've always wanted to do that with someone special."

He reached across the table and took my hand. "Am I special to you, Emily?"

Before I could answer the waitress appeared. "Hello, my name is Kim, and I'll be your server tonight. Can I start you out with a beverage?"

I wanted to reply, "Hello, I'm Emily, and I'll be your customer tonight," but I didn't. We both ordered raspberry iced tea and watched the Delta Queen.

Bob was impressed when I told him about the mystery tea parties I catered for women's groups on the Delta Queen. We held mystery tea parties at the tea room every few months, and they were so successful, the Delta Queen had hired me to present the programs there, too.

Kim brought our drinks and took our orders. Over a sumptuous meal I told Bob about Trina's overdose. It was his idea to recount everything we knew about everyone and everything. He pulled out a pen, and for lack of paper, opened a napkin to write on. In large letters he wrote the heading: Murder Case, followed by:

- Body found in Mansion. Turns out to be Pat's ex-husband and an ex-con.

Murder at the Fancy Frills Tea Room

- Trina and Sammy argue with Pat.

- Pat is murdered.

- Sammy threatens you.

- Seems to be a connection between Arthur and Sammy.

- You are harassed. Tires slashed, rock thrown through window.

- Trina overdoses on drugs. Probably supplied by Sammy.

- Arthur suddenly wants to move to Arkansas.

A slight movement behind me startled me. I looked up. Arthur was straining to read the words written on the napkin. "Playing detective?" he asked.

Bob swiftly folded the napkin and stuck it in his pocket. "It always helps to see things in black and white."

"Things aren't always the way they seem," Arthur smiled at me.

"Like that chair of yours. Who would have guessed that box of spokes and splinters you gave me could turn into a fine chair. It's just about finished, Arthur," Bob smiled cheerfully at the man whose name was on our list of suspicious characters. Had Arthur seen it?

"Wonderful!" Arthur said to Bob. Then he turned to me. "By the way, Emily, I was enjoying some classical Opera at my shop today. Then I remembered you mentioned that you could hear things through the walls. I hope I wasn't playing it so loudly that it disturbed you."

The Holy Spirit rang a warning bell in my spirit. "Didn't hear a thing," I answered. Why was Arthur suddenly concerned with the acoustics? Unless he had something to hide.

Arthur returned to the bar. "I wonder how long he was standing in back of me before we noticed him." Bob looked concerned.

"Do you think he saw his name on the list?" The food on my plate no longer interested me.

"I don't know. But I'm glad that you're staying at Liz and Roger's place now."

The promise of a romantic evening with Bob vanished and the cares of unsolved murders settled around my shoulders like a cape of doom.

✳✳✳✳✳

I was a little late getting to the shop the next morning. Liz wouldn't let me leave the breakfast table till I'd told her every word that had been spoken the previous night. I admit having breakfast on her beautiful patio, overlooking the river, made it easy to linger over a second cup of English Breakfast tea.

The scent of freshly baked scones filled the air as I opened the door to the Tea Room. Helga was a true Godsend! She was bustling about in the kitchen, her cheeks rosy from the oven's heat. She looked happy as a lark, doing what she loved to do. My pleasure turned to suspicion when my eyes fell on a huge bouquet of flowers. "Are these from Frank?" I demanded as I searched for a card.

"Ya," Helga grinned.

"Well, I don't want them. When is he going to get the message that I don't want to see him anymore?" I plucked them out of the vase and headed for the trash can.

"But, but they're -" Helga stammered.

"I know," I reconsidered. "They're too beautiful to throw away. You take them. Take them home with you and enjoy them there." I thrust the dripping bouquet at her.

"Ya, I will keep them," she beamed. I congratulated myself that my sudden burst of generosity had made her so happy.

It was late afternoon when Sheriff Doyle strode in. Two ladies were lingering over tea, so I ushered him into the side alcove. We could talk privately there, and I could still keep an eye on my customers.

I offered him tea. "I'll pass on that, but I'll take a bottle of water," he answered.

He took a long drink and then began. "Trina's out of the hospital and on her way to a rehab facility."

"Oh, I'm so glad she's alright." I couldn't help but feel sorry for her.

"We had a long talk, after she got clean," he continued. "She really wants to get off drugs and get her life together."

"She'll need to make some changes in her life. Like the kind of people she chooses for friends." I was thinking of Sammy in particular.

"We could charge her with possession of drugs, but we kind of made a deal. She's willing to testify that Sammy's a drug dealer. She also told us that he's in trouble with his suppliers. He owes them a lot of money, and they were coming down hard on him."

"That's why they tried to get money from Pat," I exclaimed. "It all makes sense now."

"There's more. Once she started talking, she couldn't stop. She said it was a relief to be able to tell someone." He took another swig of water. "She's been scared of Sammy ever since the funeral. She's pretty sure he killed Pat, and he threatened to kill her, if she didn't keep her mouth shut. Between the drugs and the threats, she was pretty much under his control."

"But if she thought he killed her Mother, why wouldn't she turn him in?" I couldn't fathom it.

"Drugs will do funny things to you. He kept her drugged and terrorized her. She explained everything to me. When she got the news that her mother had been killed, she questioned Sammy. He went into a rage, and nearly killed her." He frowned as he spoke.

"How terrible," I said, remembering the look in Sammy's eyes when he threatened me.

"We have a warrant out for his arrest. In the meantime, Trina's safe in rehab."

"Well, looks like that mystery is solved," I said as the Sheriff stood to leave. "Do you think Sammy had something to do with the other murder?"

"That's what I intend to find out. You take care of yourself, hear?" He headed for the door.

"I certainly will, "I promised.

Murder at the Fancy Frills Tea Room

My cell phone rang just as I was closing up the tea room for the day. I smiled with relief as I identified the caller as Bob, not Frank.

"Hi, are you ready?" he asked.

"Ready?" I echoed. My mind searched through our last conversation. Did I forget a date? Hard to imagine I'd forget a date with Bob!

"Ready for me to pick you up and take you to dinner. You said you liked to do things on the spur of the moment."

I grinned. He sounded so happy. "I'm still at the tea room. I was just closing up. Can you give a gal twenty minutes to freshen up?"

"Sure. I'll pick you up at Liz's," he answered.

"What a nice surprise! I'll hurry," I promised. I threw my bag in the back seat and drove to Liz's as quickly as I could. For once, all the traffic lights were in my favor, and I was there in no time at all.

Liz met me at the door, with an iced tea. "I thought you'd be home soon, so I made iced tea for all of us. There's some cheese and crackers out on the patio, if Roger hasn't eaten them all."

"That's sweet of you, Liz, but Bob's picking me up in just a few minutes, and I want to freshen up, real fast." I was moving down the hall as I talked. "And I have to feed Crumpet, too."

I tore off the shirt with the strawberry jam stain on it, and hurried to the bathroom. A few minutes later I had a fresh face on, and was pawing through the clothes hanging in the closet. "What to wear, what to wear," I muttered. I had no idea where we were going or how to dress, and I hadn't moved all my clothes over to Liz's house. I decided dressy casual, and pulled on my black capris and a black and white top. I could only find one white sandal, and finally in desperation, gave up the search. I slipped on the black sandals with a spike heel. I must have been out of my mind to bring those shoes. I seldom wore them.

When the doorbell rang, Liz got to the door before me, and was all gushy over Bob. She pulled him through the entrance. "How nice to see you again. Won't you join us out on the patio? The sunset is going to be beautiful."

"Sorry, sounds like fun, but I've got a delivery to make before I take Emily to dinner. We'll have to hurry to get there before closing."

"I'm ready," I called out as I rushed to the door. "Some other time, Liz." We headed out. I could tell she was disappointed. I turned to smile and wave, and nearly fell of those darn spike heels. Bob caught me by the arm.

"Steady there. By the way, you look very nice." He smiled down at me. His eyes seemed to sparkle with a new light.

"That's because I am nice," I teased.

He helped me up into the truck. I couldn't help but notice a large piece of furniture in the back, securely covered with some sort of tarpaulin.

"Is that the delivery?" Dumb question. What did I think it was? Table for two, complete with candelabra? "Where are you taking it?"

"It's Arthur's chair. I thought you might like to see the finished product, since you saw it when it was just a box of broken pieces." He closed the door, and went around to the driver's side.

I didn't like the idea of visiting Arthur, but it would be nice to see the restored chair. I didn't want to hurt Bob's feelings, so I didn't protest.

I held the door as Bob carried the chair into Arthur's shop. He heard us come in, and hurried out from the back room. He wore a pale cream shirt and brown tie, and was hastily pulling on a light weight tan blazer. There was a slight chemical smell in the air.

"Well, hello!" he beamed as his eyes fell upon the tarp covered chair.

I tried to help undo the cords, but I seemed to just be in the way, as Bob deftly untied the knots and the tarp fell away. Arthur and I both gasped, and Bob laughed at our astonishment.

"It's beautiful" I said. "Can I touch it?" I stepped forward, over the tarp and cords.

"Better not. It might fall apart," he warned.

I stopped short.

"Of course, you can touch it," he grinned. "It's as sturdy, if not sturdier, than the day it was made. You can even sit in it."

"Bob, you've done an amazing job. Truly, a work of art," Arthur said as he circled the chair, examining it carefully. "Try it out, Emily, I'll take a picture of you sitting in it." He took a cell phone-camera out of his pocket.

I gingerly sat in the chair, and smiled for the camera.

"It looks even better with you in it, don't you agree, Bob?" Arthur was flirting with me again.

"The words 'Pretty as a picture' come to mind," Bob agreed. "We better run along now. I promised Emily dinner."

"Just send me a bill for the chair, Bob. By the way, I'll probably have another piece or two for you to refinish next week. I want everything to be in tip top shape for the next owner."

"Have you had any prospects, yet?" I asked.

"Well, no, not yet. But it hasn't been on the market long. I hope something happens soon, though, so I can join Sue in Arkansas."

"What if -" I began, but Bob cut me off.

"Come on, Emily, we'll be late for our reservations."

Reservations? He hadn't mentioned reservations before. I thought this was a spur of the moment thing. He probably doesn't want me questioning Arthur, and making him suspicious.

"Right!" I got up out of the chair, but when I tried to take a step forward, I lost my balance. My heel had snagged on the tarp, and I could feel myself falling. I tried to clutch something to stop my ungraceful descent, but there was only thin air. I sprawled out on the floor, thankful I hadn't broken any antique vases on my way down. Bet they didn't think I was 'Pretty as a picture' now.

"Emily! Are you alright?" Bob was trying to help me sit up.

"Can you stand?" Arthur asked.

Murder at the Fancy Frills Tea Room

My left shoe had come off and was still embedded in the tarp. A sharp pain shot through my ankle as Bob helped me to my feet.

"My ankle! I think it's broken," I wailed.

"I'll call 911," Arthur said as he moved toward the phone.

"No, I'll take her to the emergency room," Bob said, examining my ankle. "Do you have any ice, Arthur? It'll keep the swelling down, till we get there."

"In the back room." He rushed through the open door to get ice for my rapidly swelling ankle.

"I don't think it's broken," Bob said as he gently felt my ankle. "But, I don't think you'll be able to go to the dance, at the country club, this week-end."

There were tears in my eyes. I'm not sure if they were from the pain, the embarrassment or that I couldn't go to the dance. I had even bought a new dress.

Arthur came back with ice wrapped in a towel. "What a shame. Since Sue's out of town, I was hoping to snag a dance or two with you myself."

The ice felt good against my throbbing ankle. I looked up at Bob. "Do I have to go to the emergency room? Maybe it will get better by itself."

"You need to get an x-ray," and with that, he picked me up and carried me to the front door. I felt like Scarlet O'Hara in a scene from Gone With the Wind. For a few seconds I even forgot about the pain in my ankle.

Arthur scurried ahead to open the door, and followed us out to the truck. He handed me my shoe, not that I'd every wear those darn spike heels again!

After a long wait in the emergency room, the x-ray finally revealed a severely sprained ankle, but nothing broken. I was instructed to RICE it. When I looked blank, the nurse explained that meant Rest, Ice and Elevate. I was given a pair of crutches, some pills for pain, and sent on my way.

I tried to apply Romans 8:38 to the evening, but for the life of me I couldn't see how anything good was going to come out of a sprained ankle, and another romantic evening ruined. I counted four blessings instead. 1. My ankle wasn't broken, 2. I had received good medical attention, 3. I had insurance to cover the bill, and 4. I was with a man who was taking very good care of me.

Instead of a gourmet dinner at the country club, we got burgers at a fast food drive through, fries and soft drinks. Then Bob drove to Liz's and helped me hobble through the door.

Chapter 19

"In everything give thanks…" I said aloud as I awkwardly climbed into my car the next morning. *"Thank you, Lord, that it's the left ankle that I sprained. At least I can drive."* I think.

Helga was already there, watering the flowers in the window boxes. "What has happened?" she sing-songed to me.

I tucked the crutches under my arms and navigated the curb. "Just a sprained ankle," I said. "Can you grab my purse for me?"

"Ya. We have a busy day, too." She frowned.

"I've already called Marcie, and Liz may come in, too, for a few hours, if she can." I tried to reassure her that my calamity would not cause a crisis for her.

"I'll just work on paperwork today, and handle the phone calls. I hope Frank doesn't call again."

"Maybe he'll come to visit instead," she said as she held the door open for me.

The sight of my tea room cheered me up immediately. It looked warm and inviting. I hoped it reflected the peace and love that God had given me when I asked Jesus into my heart. I looked at Helga more closely. "Is that lipstick you're wearing?"

"Ya." She looked embarrassed. "I thought I should look nice for the customers. Is too much? I should take it off?"

"No, no. You look very pretty, Helga. It's a good color for you." She really did look nice.

Her cheeks turned as pink as her new lipstick.

"I didn't mean to embarrass you." I stumbled for the right words.

The phone rang just then. Saved by the bell. I hoped it wasn't Frank!

The morning hours flew by. I hobbled around, getting as much done as I could, while Helga worked quietly and efficiently, turning out mouth-watering pastries. Marcie came in just before the noon rush, and settled into her routine.

The door flew open. "Never fear, the Team is here!" Liz announced, as she made a grand entrance. A grinning Roger accompanied her. "I bet you didn't know I worked my way through college as a waiter," he said. He draped a white towel over his arm as proof.

"Oh, you two are a God-send. I don't know what I would do without all of you." I swept my eyes over Marcie, Helga, Liz and Roger.

Things couldn't have gone smoother if I'd hired a team from the Carlton-Ritz. Marcie and Roger waited on tables, Liz helped Helga in the kitchen, and I sat at a high stool at the cash register. I felt like a Queen, surveying her kingdom. I was so thankful for God's goodness to me.

The door opened again. "You look like a Queen surveying her kingdom," Arthur said as he strode in.

My tea room, my kingdom. He was right, that's exactly how I felt.

"How's the ankle?"

"Fine, just fine." If only it would stop throbbing. "Do you want something for lunch? The special today is chicken salad in a tomato cup, and butternut squash soup. Oh, and vanilla almond scones."

Arthur rolled his eyes. "I don't suppose you could find a piece of ham or plain chicken that you could put between a couple of piece of real bread?"

I had to laugh. "I imagine Helga could put together a regular sandwich for you. Do you want it to go?"

"Yes, I've got to get back to my shop. And I wouldn't want word to get out to your other customers that you can do a ham and Swiss on rye."

Liz wiped her hands on her apron as she came in from the kitchen. "I thought I heard a man's voice out here, other than Roger's." She glared at Arthur. "What are you doing here?" Liz's demeanor was making it quite clear she was still angry with Arthur for not listing with her.

"Just getting something for his lunch, Liz," I answered as I handed her the order ticket.

"It's a take out," I called after Liz, who was already heading back to the kitchen.

Customers continued to come and go.

"Hey, how's my girl?" It was Bob. I could tell, without looking up, by the pounding of my heart at the sound of his voice.

"I'm fine," I smiled. I felt lots better now that he was here. "Gosh, three men in my tea room, all at the same time. I think that's a record."

"Well, I just hope no one sees me. That's why I'm wearing sun glasses and a baseball cap," he grinned.

"I'm only here because I'm doing my good deed for the day, "Roger chimed in. "Soon as I'm out of here, I'm heading for the practice range." He mimicked a swing with an imaginary golf club. "I got a new driver I'm anxious to practice with. It's a Ping with trajectory tuning. I can't wait to try it out."

"He's so proud of that club, he practically sleeps with it," Liz complained as she plunked Arthur's take out on the counter.

"Hello, Bob." Her greeting to Bob was in stark contrast to the coldness in her voice when she spoke to Arthur. "Will we see you at the Country Club dance tonight?" she asked Bob.

I held my breath, waiting for his answer. Would he go to the dance without me?

"Well, since Twinkle Toes is out of commission, guess I'll catch up on some work at the shop. I've got a rush custom job that I need to get out as soon as possible, so looks like I'll be burning the midnight oil on the shop floor instead of the dance floor." He looked down at my ankle.

Arthur paid for his lunch, and turned at the door. "Take care of that ankle, Emily."

"I know. Rest, elevate and ice. That's how I plan on spending the evening," I replied.

He was barely out of earshot, when Liz said. "I don't know how you can be so nice to him, when he lied to the Sheriff about you and that knife."

"I don't understand why he did that, either," I looked up at Bob. "Maybe he just made an honest mistake. I can't believe Arthur would do anything, intentionally, to hurt me."

"But he has done some strange things lately," Roger warned.

"Maybe he's having a midlife crisis. Like you did, Roger, remember?" Liz elbowed him.

"You mean when I wanted to buy an interest in the Fairwoods Golf Course? We'd have made a fortune on that deal, but oh, no, you couldn't agree with me." He snapped his towel at her.

"It's a good thing I stuck to my guns, too. If you remember, my dear, that was the year we had so much rain, the greens were underwater for weeks on end," Liz gloated.

"Yes, I remember. I had to drive clear over to Lincoln County to play any golf." He took another swing with his imaginary Ping.

"Come on, help me finish up in the back," Liz led Roger thru the kitchen door. "The customers are all gone, and I just have a thing or two to do before I can leave. I have to get my hair done for tonight."

"You look gorgeous just as you are," Roger teased, as he planted a kiss on her cheek.

Helga was walking past the phone, just as it rang. I nodded at her, and she picked it up. "Fancy Frills Tea Room," she said in her Minnesota accent .

"Ya, it is." She turned away from Bob and I.

"Oh, ya, I would like that." She spoke very softly. I couldn't hear what she said, but then she giggled into the phone. I'd never heard Helga giggle before. If I didn't know better, I'd think she was talking to a boyfriend. "Ya." Long pause. "Ya, I will be ready." She was smiling as she hung up the phone. "It was for me," she explained sheepishly.

"A heavy date?" I loved teasing her. My words had the intended result.

She was blushing. "Ya, Well, maybe. I don't know!" She headed back to the safety of the kitchen.

"Love is in the air, it seems," Bob's gaze on me was steady.

"Yes, it does seem that way," I returned his gaze. I was thinking of us, not Helga.

He broke the moment first. "Well, I just dropped by to see how you're doing. I better get going. I have to run over to the lumber yard, and then get busy on that custom order."

"Right," I gathered together the stack of receipts as I spoke. "I'll be finishing up here soon, too. My ankle tells me it's had enough of a workout today. It's time for rest, ice and elevation.

*****

I knew Liz and Roger would be having dinner at the country club and I didn't want Liz to have to think about what to feed her star boarder. Anyway, that was the excuse I used to rationalize my stop at In and Out drive through when I finally left the shop hours later. I ordered my favorite burger and fries and iced tea.

I parked in the parking lot to eat. It was easier to eat in the car than to go inside. I wasn't very adept at using the crutches, especially if I tried to carry something at the same time. After all, it was my gracefulness that had gotten me into this predicament in the first place. I settled back in the car seat, gave thanks for the food I was about to enjoy, and tried to ignore the pain in my ankle. There's nothing like a good burger to take your mind off your troubles.

I let my mind wander as I ate and watched the cars go by. I nearly choked as I saw a beat up blue truck whiz down the avenue. Sammy! No, it couldn't be. Even Sammy wouldn't be stupid enough to drive through town in broad daylight. Did Sammy's truck have a dent in the side, like the truck I just saw? I didn't think so, it was just a case of nerves, I told myself.

✵✵✵✵✵

Liz came down the steps looking dazzling. She was wearing enough bling to light up Vegas. She wore a tight, long, red dress that sparkled different shades of red as she moved.

"Bold and beautiful, that's the way I like my women," Roger said, as he met her at the bottom of the steps. He reluctantly placed his new Ping driver in his golf bag, by the door, ready for his next practice session.

"Are you sure you'll be alright, all by yourself, sweetie?" Liz said as she preened in the hall mirror.

"I'll be fine, "I reassured her. "I've got plenty of ice, the phone is right here, next to the TV remote, and I've even got some magazines. I can catch up on some reading."

"And she'll be guarded by that ferocious attack cat, Crumpet," Roger added.

The attack cat was already curled up on my lap, enjoying sentinel duty. I knew of course, that my real security came from the Lord. "The Lord is my helper, I will not be afraid. What can man do to me?" (Hebrews 13:6 NIV) I quoted. I was soon to find out.

*****

It was English humor night on TV, and some of those English sitcoms are my favorite shows. I consoled myself that if I had to be stuck at home with my iced foot propped up on several pillows, at least I could spend the evening with some of my favorite English characters. I munched on potato chips, and tried not to feel sorry for myself. My thoughts soon turned to Bob and I wondered if he might call. My eyes grew heavy and I started to doze, as the pain pill, I took earlier, kicked in.

I was startled when the doorbell rang. Could Liz and Roger be home already? No, it was probably Liz, coming back to check on me. It would be just like her. I bet she forgot her keys, again. She's always misplacing them. Now I had to get up and answer the door. Thanks a lot, Liz!

I hobbled to the door, feeling groggy, and leaning heavily on one crutch. "Did you forget your keys again?" I asked as I opened the door.

I gasped in shock. "Oh, it's you!"

Arthur pushed open the door, and stepped inside, almost knocking me over.

"Is Bob here?" He looked right past me, his eyes sweeping over the downstairs.

Before I could answer, Sammy lunged in from his hiding place in the bushes, and knocked me off balance.

Arthur quickly shut the door, and yelled at Sammy. "I told you to wait till we knew she was alone." I'd never seen Arthur look so threatening, so mean. Where was the flirtatious, suave Arthur I'd always known?

"What's going on?" I tried to act like I wasn't afraid, and clear my groggy head. "'*Jesus, help me,*'" I silently pleaded.

"You were warned, Emily. It's a pity you couldn't stay out of things," Arthur said.

"What are you talking about?" I kept backing up, and he kept moving toward me.

"The sooner we get this over with, the better," Sammy said, as he pulled a gun out of his jacket and pointed it at me. That's when I noticed a button was missing from his jacket.

"Nothing personal, Emily. I like you, I really do." Arthur reached out and caressed my hair. I recoiled at his touch. "What a pity it has to end this way. But you know too much, I'm afraid." He smiled sympathetically.

"I don't know what you're talking about, Arthur. I – I don't know anything." I glanced around the room. Could I make it to the andiron at the fireplace?

"Oh, come now. You're much too smart to play dumb. Too smart for your own good. You put two and two together, too many times. First you put the two murders together. Then you discovered there was a connection between Sammy and I. Then you learned about the counterfeit money in town, and when you saw the printing press in the back room, you added it all up."

I couldn't believe this was happening. A voice in my head said to stall for time. Time for what?

Sammy's hand was shaking and his pupils were dilated. He danced from one foot to another, waving the gun in my direction. "Get out of the way, so I can shoot her. I'll take care of her just like I took care of that old biddy."

"You're wrong about me, Arthur. I don't know what you're talking about. I have no idea why you or anyone would have killed Pat!"

"Oh, don't look so innocent. I'm sure you figured out that Pat had to be eliminated because she knew about the counterfeit plates. Seems her ex had written her a letter from prison, telling her the plates were hidden in the old Harwood mansion. He even told her how to get in through the old tunnel they used back in prohibition days, and that if anything happened to him, she should tell the police.

When she heard he'd been found dead out there, she went to see if the plates were still there. Too bad for her, Sammy was out there that day, too. He'd gone back to make sure he hadn't overlooked anything."

"You mean Sammy killed Pat's ex to get the counterfeit plates?" It was beginning to make sense to me now.

I saw a flash of red out of the corner of my eye and heard Sammy yelp. The gun dropped to the floor as Liz hit him a second time with Roger's brand new golf club. Sammy fell to the floor in a heap.

As Arthur turned to see what was going on, I grabbed a poker from the andiron and nailed him across the head. He collapsed like a wet noodle, all class and dignity gone. I lost my balance and nearly toppled on top of him, but I caught myself on the winged back chair.

"Call 911!" Liz yelled. She had hiked up her tight dress, and had straddled an unconscious Sammy. She held the golf club, ready to clobber him again, if he regained consciousness.

I picked up the gun and held it in Arthur's direction. I'd never held a gun before, and I was surprised how steady my hand was. With my other hand, I punched in the number on the phone.

Sheriff Doyle and Bear arrived within minutes. Bear helped Liz remove herself from Sammy's unconscious form, and politely looked the other way as she tugged her dress back into place.

Sammy and Arthur were both busy accusing each other as Bear handcuffed them. The Sheriff would have no trouble getting full confessions out of either one of them. They were led out to a waiting police car.

"Sammy killed both Pat and her ex-husband," I began breathlessly. "And Arthur's a counterfeiter! That wasn't an antique press I saw in his shop, it was for printing counterfeit money."

"Better sit down, and try to calm yourself, Emily," the Sheriff said, directing me to a chair. I was babbling and, now that it was over, shaking like a leaf. "We'll get statements from all of you in the morning."

Murder at the Fancy Frills Tea Room

✳✳✳✳✳

The story made headlines in the newspaper the next day. Bob, Roger, Liz and I poured over the details as we drank iced tea on her patio. We had just returned from giving statements at the police station.

"It's a good thing Roger had his golf bag right at the front door, ready to play the next morning," Liz said, as she sipped her tea.

"Yes," I agreed, "but why did you come back to the house? Did you forget something again?"

"No, it wasn't me this time," Liz explained. Roger forgot his credit cards. His tux was so tight, he couldn't get his wallet in the pocket. He intended to slip a single credit card in his pocket, but he forgot to do it. So, I offered to go back and get it for him. Of course, I wanted to check on you, too. When I saw Sammy's truck parked down the street, I got suspicious. So, I just snuck in the front door and grabbed the nearest weapon I could find."

"I hope you didn't dent Roger's new driver," I said.

"Sammy's got a hard head," Liz answered. We all laughed.

"Now, let me see if I have this straight," Bob said. Sammy and the Johnson guy were in prison together. That's how Sammy found out about the plates. Right?"

I shook my head yes.

"So he got out of prison before Johnson and waited for him at the mansion. When Johnson came for the plates, he killed him. Sammy found out that Arthur could only print small bills on the plates he had, and worked out a deal with him. He'd provide the plates for large denomination bills, Arthur would print the money, and they'd split the pot.

Then, when Sammy found Pat out there, he shot her, too. He told the Sheriff he dragged her body out to her car and dumped it in the trunk. He drove her car to Westport, hoping people wouldn't connect the two murders."

I shook my head again. "Poor Pat. If only she'd gone to the police before she went out to the mansion, looking for the plates." I remembered how upset Pat had been those last few days.

"I wonder if Arthur's wife, Sue, knew what was going on, Liz pondered.

"I heard the Sheriff tell Bear that Arthur had sent Sue away so she wouldn't find out. Seems Arthur was planning on pulling a fast one on Sammy. He was going to escape to Brazil, with the plates, as soon as he could."

"I'm so proud of you, Emily. You were so brave," Bob said, as I refilled his glass.

"It was strange. Of course, I was afraid. But a scripture came to my mind in the midst of the ordeal. "Because he loves me," says the Lord, "I will rescue him. I will protect him, for he acknowledges my name." It's from Ps 91:4.

Liz quickly replied, "Yes, but I think Ps 116:6 is more appropriate."

Bob asked, "What does that one say?"

"The Lord protects the simple hearted," Liz quoted with a wink. We all laughed.

"Oh, my gosh!" Liz exclaimed. "I don't believe it!" She had been glancing through the newspaper, as we talked.

She pointed to the column that listed wedding licenses. Frank and Helga's names were listed.

"Frank and Helga!" My mouth dropped open. All those phone calls from Frank, the flowers he sent that I almost threw away; it all began to add up. They weren't for me, they were for Helga! It seems I had been an unknowing matchmaker. I had Helga answer his phone calls, and visit with him, while I stayed busy in the back room, and love had bloomed. I was ecstatic for Helga, but I had to admit, my ego took a blow.

I couldn't wait to see Helga the next day and congratulate her. Her eyes were bright with excitement, and she was humming as she worked.

"Ya, it is all so sudden. We are very happy." She pronounced 'happy' to sound like 'hoppy' and I had an immediate word picture of Helga and Frank hopping down the bunny trail of matrimony. I brought myself back to reality.

She continued on, raising a cloud of flour as she kneaded fancy yeast dough. "Everyone is so nice. So many calls already, telling us how happy they are for us." There was that hoppy picture again. "Even an invitation from that Mrs. Jean Wilcox, inviting us to dinner. So nice she is. She want to show us big plan to save money, be healthy and live long time."

The phone rang. It was Liz.

"Hey, I've got a new client and I'm going out to the Harwood place. Do you want to come along? I promise to bring the key!"

The End

About the Author

Maxine Holmgren is a Christian author, playwright and entrepreneur. She lives in Southern California with her husband, who is an avid golfer and golf instructor.

She is grateful to the Lord for giving her the talent and skill to write. She has used this gift to combine her passion for tea, mysteries, and acting by writing short stories, party plans, plays, and now, a Christian mystery novel.

Writing *mystery tea party plans* for friends was the natural outlet for her talents. This soon led to an internet business. Her humorous *mystery party plans* are sold nationally, and even internationally, at www.mysteryteaparties.com .

Maxine Holmgren

Maxine enjoys public speaking and does presentations to women's groups, about the health benefits of tea. She also belongs to an amateur theatre group where she enjoys acting and directing.

In addition to the sixteen *mystery tea party plans*, she has also written four one act comedies that have been published and are listed in the **Samuel French Catalogue of Plays**.
www.samuelfrench.com

She says, "I like to include as much humor as possible, when I write. I think we all need more laughter in our lives. 'A merry heart doeth good, like a medicine.' (Prov.17:22)"

More from Maxine!

Mystery Tea Party Plans available on

<u>www.mysteryteaparties.com</u>

- ➤ **Who Killed the Darling Duke of Darjeeling?**
  Who did the dastardly deed of doing away with the dreadful Duke?

- ➤ **The Bodacious Babes of Buzzard Bend**
  Who killed Calhoun Cahootz? A rootin', tootin' mystery set in the wild, wild, West.

- ➤ **Who Killed the Roving Romeo of the Red Feather Ladies?**
  Who double crossed the double crosser before the double crosser crossed her?

- ➤ **The Red Feather Ladies Aboard The S.S. Titantica**
  A sequel to the Roving Romeo. There's more than tea brewing out at sea. This calls for scrutiny on the bounty.

- ➤ **Sherla Combs and the Case of the Great Jewel Robberies**
  Can Sherla Combs and her sidekick, Dr. Whatstone, discover the thief?

- ➤ **The Decadent Housewives of Hysteria Lane**
  Which trouble making neighbor made trouble for the neighbor?

- ➤ **Who Stole the Joy From Christmas?**
  A Christian Christmas tea party plan. Forget the

holiday frenzy and focus on the real meaning of Christmas.

➢ **Murder at the Earl of Grey's Hound Manor**
Guests gather for the reading of the will. Will the murderer get what she deserves?

➢ **Who's Missing From the Class Reunion?**
A Christian mystery. Guests attend the class reunion of 19??

➢ **Mayhem on Maui**
Was there poison in the punch of the pineapple plantation proprietor?

➢ **The Case of the Crazy Quilt Caper**
Who stole Grandma's prize winning quilt? The $100,000 prize is at stake.

➢ **Gone With the Breeze**
Which Southern belle has stolen the mortgage money for Kara Plantation?

➢ **The Sinister Sleepover**
Which guest spent the night committing robbery and murder?

➢ **The Case of the Missing Artwork**
For children 8 and over. Who drew upon their creativity and became an art thief?

➢ **Who Stole the Wedding Bells?**
Who would want to stop the wedding? Perfect for a wedding shower.

➢ **The Missing Christmas Tree**
How does a huge community Christmas tree disappear? It's a mystery!

Stage plays available on
www.SAMUELFRENCH.com

Christian Mystery novels available on
www.AMAZON.com
in paperback and KINDLE.

Ten reasons to drink tea

1. Tea relaxes and lowers stress because of the ingredient L-thianine. Tea is the only plant in the world, except for one rare mushroom, that contains this amazing substance.

2.   Drinking any kind of true tea, with its super ingredient L-thianine lowers stress, which lowers cortisol, thus decreasing formation of belly fat.

3. Green tea naturally contains vitamins B1, B2, B6, K, C and folic acid.

4. Tea contains polyphenols that contain more antioxidant activity than vitamins C and E.

5. New studies show that it may help prevent rheumatoid arthritis and/or lessen the pain in those already suffering from it.

6. Tea is good for the heart because it helps to lower blood pressure. One study showed drinking tea daily may lower the risk of high blood pressure by nearly 50 percent.

7. Since the 1990's hundreds of studies have been performed showing that tea can inhibit the formation of cancer tumors, and slow the growth of those already formed.

8. Black tea helps relax and expand arteries, which increases blood flow to the heart.

9. Tea contains fluoride which fights bacteria that causes gum disease and tooth decay.

10. Tea contains polyphenols that helps to remove free radicals which helps to delay aging of the skin such as dark spots and wrinkles.

For best results, drink at least four cups of tea a day.

Made in the USA
Charleston, SC
03 February 2014